The
Woman
Priest

Anonymous portrait of Sylvain Maréchal. The engraving is taken from a bust of Maréchal, which was modeled in turn on the death-mask made by his friend and fellow author, Mme. Gacon-Dufour. The portrait appeared in the 1807 edition of Maréchal's De la vertu. *(Courtesy Université de Montréal.)*

The Woman Priest

A Translation of Sylvain Maréchal's Novella, La femme abbé

Translation and Introduction by Sheila Delany

The University of Alberta Press

Published by

The University of Alberta Press
Ring House 2
Edmonton, Alberta, Canada T6G 2E1
www.uap.ualberta.ca

Copyright © 2016 Translation, Introduction
and annotations, Sheila Delany.

LIBRARY AND ARCHIVES CANADA
CATALOGUING IN PUBLICATION

Maréchal, Sylvain, 1750–1803
[Femme abbé. English]
    The woman priest : a translation of
Sylvain Maréchal's Novella,
La femme abbé / translation and
introduction by Sheila Delany.

Includes bibliographical references.
Issued in print and electronic formats.
ISBN 978-1-77212-123-0 (paperback).—
ISBN 978-1-77212-289-3 (PDF). —
ISBN 978-1-77212-287-9 (EPUB). —
ISBN 978-1-77212-288-6 (MOBI)

    I. Delany, Sheila, writer of introduction,
translator II. Title. III. Title: Femme abbé.
English.

PQ2001.M5F413 2016   843'.5
C2016-901935-7
C2016-901936-5

First edition, first printing, 2016.
Printed and bound in Canada by Houghton
Boston Printers, Saskatoon, Saskatchewan.
Copyediting and proofreading by
Joanne Muzak.

All rights reserved. No part of this publication
may be reproduced, stored in a retrieval
system, or transmitted in any form or by any
means (electronic, mechanical, photocopying,
recording, or otherwise) without prior
written consent. Contact the University of
Alberta Press for further details.

The University of Alberta Press supports
copyright. Copyright fuels creativity, encourages diverse voices, promotes free speech,
and creates a vibrant culture. Thank you for
buying an authorized edition of this book
and for complying with the copyright laws by
not reproducing, scanning, or distributing
any part of it in any form without permission. You are supporting writers and allowing
University of Alberta Press to continue to
publish books for every reader.

The University of Alberta Press is committed
to protecting our natural environment.
As part of our efforts, this book is printed
on Enviro Paper: it contains 100% post-
consumer recycled fibres and is acid- and
chlorine-free.

The University of Alberta Press gratefully
acknowledges the support received for its
publishing program from the Government
of Canada, the Canada Council for the Arts,
and the Government of Alberta through the
Alberta Media Fund.

Contents

VII   *Acknowledgments*
IX   *Introduction*
XXXIII   *Translator's Note*

1   The Woman Priest

61   *Notes*
65   *Bibliography*

Acknowledgments

THIS TRANSLATION was initially made from the Project Gutenberg ebook *La femme abbé*, file 23098-8.txt; my gratitude to the Gutenberg team (Laurent Vogel, Hugo Voisard, and Christine P. Travers) for making it and many other early modern texts available for study and enjoyment. Later I was able to consult the illustrated copy held at Yale's Beinecke Rare Books and Manuscript Library. Professor Erica Mannucci of Milan, fellow admirer of Sylvain, offered important details on the Canadian connection. My thanks to John Craig, dean of arts at Simon Fraser University, for his support of the project via the Retirees Grant, Faculty of Arts and Social Sciences; and to the University Publications Fund. The indispensable Ivana Niseteo and Vera Yuen at Simon Fraser's library have helped me, as always, with searches and databases. To my two readers for the University of Alberta Press, much appreciation for your microscopic work on the translation and Introduction, and for suggestions that have made this a better book. Thanks as well to Joanne Muzak, copyeditor extraordinaire, for her careful attention to everything.

This is the second in a set of three translations of Maréchal's work that I plan. The first, of his satirical legendary *La nouvelle légende dorée* (1790), was published by the University of Alberta Press in 2012 as *Anti-Saints:* The New Golden Legend *of Sylvain Maréchal*; the third will be of his careful, rationalistic study of

Hebrew and Christian scripture, *Pour et contre la Bible* (For and against the Bible, 1801). These are the works that interested me most among Maréchal's voluminous production, not least because their themes of religion, sex, and politics remain so current in our private and public lives. For the research underlying all my work on Maréchal and his period, I am indebted to Canada's Social Sciences and Humanities Research Council and to Simon Fraser University for grants that enabled me to work at Stanford, Berkeley, Columbia, Yale, and the New York Public Library.

Introduction

CROSS-DRESSING: surely, we may think, a contemporary phenomenon, a product of our mixed-up times. But far from it: there it is in indigenous North American tribal culture with the berdache or two-spirit person; in European medieval saints' lives and high-medieval French *contes* and *fabliaux*; in Arabic cultures; in the Indian "third-sex" hijra communities;[1]—and in the social reality of Sylvain Maréchal's day in France and elsewhere, as we will see below. Before and after Maréchal's time, some girls and women passed as men in order to serve as sailors or soldiers or even pirates. Even today, stories continue to surface of women passing as men to acquire enhanced opportunities, and girls dressing or being dressed as boys for protection.[2]

It may be difficult for us to imagine the shock value of his title—*La femme abbé*, the woman priest—at a time when the Catholic ban on women's ordination was accepted by a majority of France's population and indeed that of Europe, and when other denominations had not yet opened the way for women officiants as they have in recent years, when we see women rabbis, cantors, ministers, and bishops. Maréchal's story of a cross-dressing girl was probably less scandalous to a contemporary audience than what he has her do: study Latin on her own, apply to and be admitted into an elite Parisian seminary, take minor orders, and serve as private clerk-secretary to the handsome young priest, Saint-Almont, with whom she is obsessed. Indeed, so efficiently does the star-struck Agatha perform her duties that the next step in her successful ecclesiastical career can only be admission to full priesthood with all its sacerdotal obligations, such as hearing confession or performing marriage and the other sacraments. All of this, of course (except the learning of Latin), was forbidden to women by centuries-long policy of the Catholic Church. It still is as I write this in 2015, though not without protest from many in the Church, both men and women, lay and ordained.

Although raised as a Catholic, Sylvain Maréchal (1750–1803) early on became a militant atheist, enemy not only of the Catholic Church (the dominant religious institution in the France of his day) but of all religion—or, as he would have it, "superstition" whether Christian, Jewish, Muslim, or other. His own faith was in nature and reason. He left law school for ethical reasons and because his stutter would disqualify him from the oratory required in that profession. Instead, he devoted himself to literature both as reader and writer in many genres ranging from classicizing erotic lyric to impassioned political treatise. Committed to domestic harmony, he married an observant Catholic woman considerably younger than himself in a religious ceremony, wrote erotic verse to her, and apparently lived happily with her until his death in 1803, when he was buried by a priest in a church cemetery. His nickname for his wife was Zoé—Greek for "life"—the same name he gives to Agatha's sensible and happily married confidante.

Maréchal's sardonic anti-establishment writing, as expressed in his *Almanach des honnêtes gens* (1788), landed him in prison for a short time; the volume was publicly burnt by order of Parlement as an offense to morals and taste. It had, however, a *succès de scandale* and earned him a modest fortune. Moreover, its calendrical format, typical of the almanac genre, along with its rationalist-humanist content, made it a model for what a few years later would become the new revolutionary calendar. Maréchal welcomed the great French Revolution of 1789 and, as editor of and writer for the influential Parisian journal *Révolutions de Paris* from about 1790 to its demise in early 1794, he was able to spread the news across the country. His play *Le jugement dernier des rois* (1793) depicted the ignominious deaths of a group of tyrannical kings and a pope; it was a hit in Paris and other major cities and was supported by the revolutionary government.

As a librarian in the prestigious Mazarin Library in Paris, Maréchal had access to a vast treasury of manuscripts and books from every period; even before taking up this position, he had been well schooled in the classics. The fruit of his study, whether while employed at the Mazarin or before or afterward, is obvious in the breadth of reference in his many works, ranging from classical Greek and Roman through medieval and Renaissance, and international in scope. He would have encountered the phenomenon of cross-dressing in many texts, some of them rare, some readily available. When his heroine, Agatha, remarks in Letter XIII that she has several antecedents for her daring transgressive project, she may well have in mind—Maréchal certainly did—some of the cross-dressing saints whose stories, well known over the centuries, disseminated in sermons, almanacs, and popular pamphlets, were also amply represented in the Mazarin holdings of hagiographical literature. Those who appear in Maréchal's 1790 set of women saints' lives, the satirical *Nouvelle légende dorée* (*New Golden Legend*) include Eugenia, Euphrosyne, Hildegonde, Marina, and Pelagia (see Delany, *Anti-Saints*).

But the phenomenon was far from merely literary, especially during the period of the Revolution. Every French person would know of Joan of Arc who, though not canonized until the twentieth century, was a national heroine for her military leadership of French forces against the English in the fifteenth century. She had, of course, dressed as a man; this was one of the offenses for which she was tried and executed. So, too, did some Frenchwomen dress as men to perform military service in Maréchal's day. Despite being excluded from the franchise and from holding office (an injustice against which many women and men strongly protested), women had political discussion clubs (until these were shut down by the Robespierre government late in 1793), newspapers, and magazines, and they played a leadership role both verbally and physically in many major struggles. When women joined the ranks of either the revolutionary army or its counterrevolutionary enemies, they often did so dressed as men or passing as men, sometimes to be unmasked only when taken to hospital wounded or dead (Bouvier, 198–215). Even apart from the military instance, women sometimes found it convenient and liberating to wear trousers, much as Agatha does in her first forays into transvestism; enhanced employment opportunities might well play a role, especially in Holland and England (see Dekker and van de Pol). In Paris, the well-known revolutionary and feminist Théroigne de Méricourt dressed as a man in her daily peregrination around the city (Yalom, 21); the theatre critic Mme. de Beaumer did so in order to enter the cheap seats that were restricted to men (Gelbart, 95), and it is likely that, especially given the wide range of heavy-work jobs filled by women, others did the same. At the other end of the social spectrum from working women, some fashionable Parisiennes in 1799 enjoyed the thrill of donning menswear. The tendency was not ignored by the authorities, and in 1800 a new law made the fad illegal (Douthwaite, 50). Thus, Agatha's disguise, playfully endorsed by her indulgent grandma, would, by the time of the novella's publication, be not only culturally transgressive but illegal.

✶ By 1801, when *La femme abbé* was published, Maréchal was a severely disillusioned revolutionary. He saw the cause he had embraced halted partway through, unable to complete its trajectory toward the fully egalitarian society he and others had hoped for in 1789, despite the loss of millions who had died to achieve

and defend the revolution. The brave new constitution of 1793—
imperfect, but a step in the right direction—had been suspended,
permanently, as it turned out. Atheism, Maréchal's lifelong conviction, had been declared an aristocratic vice by the "incorruptible"
Robespierre, and Robespierre himself was sent to the guillo-
tine in 1794. Maréchal's friend, the radical lawyer François-Noël
("Gracchus") Babeuf, leader of a planned insurrection against
the new bourgeois government, had been betrayed and executed
in 1797. Through mere coincidence, Maréchal escaped arrest
(Dommanget, *Sur Babeuf*, Chap. 10), but it was clearly time to
keep a low profile. The government had turned the revolutionary
army, led by Napoleon, against a still more revolutionary urban
working population whose needs and demands it refused to meet.
Counterrevolutionary priests and aristocrats flocked back into
France from their exile in England as earlier attempts to reform
the Catholic Church were abandoned or reversed; even the once-
despised Pope was invited to preside over the coronation of the
new Bonaparte monarch. Clearly, the revolution (as Napoleon
proclaimed in 1797) was over.

In such a context, the two works that Maréchal published in
1801 represent a kind of farewell to the hopes and possibilities
that had sustained him since young manhood. *Pour et contre la
Bible* (*For and against the Bible*) is a close reading of Hebrew and
Christian scriptures from a critical-rationalistic perspective that
combines literary, moral, and historical approaches in a massive
critique of Judaeo-Christian tradition. Having often written on
specific institutional abuses, especially in his *Nouvelle légende
dorée*, here he analyzes the urtexts, the foundational scriptural
writings that he sees as responsible for every subsequent institutional and theological abuse. As he observes in his life of the Virgin
Mary, without her acquiescence to the angelic annunciation, we
might have had "no popes, no cardinals, no priests, no masses, no
councils, no indulgences, no inquisitions, no crusades, no Saint

Bartholomew's Day Massacre, no Carmelites, no little nuns"[3] (*La nouvelle légende*, trans. Delany). His biblical reading thus becomes a mordant message to his countrymen in the new century just begun, a century from which he and many others had hoped much more but which now Maréchal sees as, dismayingly, no improvement on previous ones.

La femme abbé, published the same year, may be taken as something of a companion piece. Though taking the more accessible form of an epistolary novella, it displays many of the same opinions both through its plot and through the opinions of the character of Timon (clearly named after the eponymous misanthrope of Shakespeare's play). Introduced late in the story as Agatha's caretaker during her last days, Timon seems to serve as something close to authorial *porte-parole*: anti-clerical, anti-religious, author of a book that brought him fame and trouble, weighed down by blasted hopes for a society governed by reason and nature. Yet Timon is capable of the most delicate charitable gestures and perceptions in his relationship with the depressed Agatha, making her comfortable, attempting to cure her broken heart, offering her a new life with him in the new world across the Atlantic.

Timon lives, and Agatha dies, in a vast subterranean cave system, actually a disused quarry located south of Paris between the villages of Ivry and Vitry-sur-Seine, as the narrator specifies. Such quarries are common beneath and around Paris, some of them now used as chic underground restaurants, mushroom farms, bomb shelters, or wine cellars. From the late Middle Ages, these quarries were a source of limestone, clay, and gypsum used to build the edifices and streets of Paris; by the later eighteenth century most of them were exhausted. Agatha stumbles across the entrance to Timon's cavern while wandering, shell-shocked and lost, in search of the River Seine where she plans to end her life. Having at last revealed the secret of her sex, she has been expelled from the seminary by the priest she is obsessed with and whose private secretary she has become. This seminary, located near Paris and only two or three hours' walk from the above-named villages, possesses a country retreat where the seminarians often go for recreation, and where Agatha makes her fatal confession. There was such a seminary in the vicinity: the well-known Parisian seminary of Saint-Sulpice with its country house at the village of Issy, a major site of chalk quarries only a few miles southwest of central Paris. Once the royal pavilion of Queen Marguerite, it was later donated to the Sulpicians as a branch of their Paris house; its luxurious grounds and copses correspond well to the description Maréchal gives of the landscape surrounding the seminarians' outing and the disastrous final interview of Agatha and Saint-Almont.

This is an area that Maréchal knew well. Having lived in Paris his entire life, first in the center and then, after his marriage in 1792 in the more rural faubourg Saint-Marceau, he later retired to the rural village of Montrouge "pour mieux voir le soleil" ("the better to see the sun": Fusil, 271). This was close to the other sites mentioned above and itself the site of quarries used, from the fifteenth century on, for construction in Paris. Here Maréchal died of natural causes in the company of his wife, his good friend the writer Mme. Gacon-Dufour, and a few other close friends.

The geographical specificity of setting is not duplicated in temporal specificity. We are told by the "editor" or "publisher" of the letters that the action takes place "well before 1789," but we are not told how long before. Saint-Almont's first Paris mass is said to be an elaborate affair, with Miroir at the organ. Miroir was prominent as a Parisian organist from about 1780, so it is tempting to think that the events are not far removed from the author's lifetime; but other details suggest that he may have had an earlier period in mind.

✳ France's colonial empire figures prominently in the novella, especially toward the end of the story. The intense correspondence between the two best friends Agatha and Zoé is interrupted when

Zoé must accompany her husband to a post overseas, as she reports in Letter XV; thus the correspondence is replaced by Agatha's diary, which she addresses to the absent Zoé. In Letter XVII, Agatha refers to her friend's "departure for the islands," even though no destination was specified in Zoé's previous letter. These islands might be the French-dominated Antilles off the Americas, between Florida and Venezuela; or the archipelago colonies of Mauritius or Seychelles, both in the vicinity of Madagascar off the southeast coast of Africa.

This represents an inconsistency that Maréchal did not correct, for later we discover that the posting was to North America, which seems to have occupied a special place in Maréchal's imagination. Timon, having allowed affection for Agatha to overcome his antisocial tendencies, suggests to her "a happy future according to his principles": he proposes that they emigrate to form a little colony "in the forests of North America…in the vicinity of the good Quakers." This would likely be Pennsylvania or Rhode Island, where Quakers established significant colonies, and could refer to any time after 1681, when William Penn received his land grant and Quakers began to emigrate to the British colonies. On returning, Zoé attempts to administer to her friend—too late, as it turns out—a medicine made by Canadian "savages" and well known for its miraculous cures. At the very end, all of the other characters beside Agatha—Timon, the priest Saint-Almont, and Zoé with her husband—wind up in "Canada." This geographical designation (as distinct from "Acadia," "Newfoundland," or "Nova Scotia") was not the entire country of Canada as we know it today. Rather, it was, and had been since the late sixteenth century, the northern part of New France, "la nouvelle-France," the vast French colonial empire in North America extending from the Gulf of Mexico northward almost to Hudson Bay, and from the Appalachians westward nearly to the Rockies—roughly half the continent. However, the French empire in North America ended with their defeat at the Battle of

Quebec (1759), also known as the Battle of the Plains of Abraham, and the subsequent Treaty of Paris (1763), which ceded control to the English. If we may assume that a French colonial administrator such as Zoé's husband would not be posted to an area under English control, then we may imagine the action taking place before this period.

The Indian population mentioned as targets of Saint-Almont's conversion efforts are the Iroquois, who were indigenous to this territory (as opposed, for instance, to Mi'kmaq in the Acadia region). The Iroquois, a confederation of five and then, after 1722, six nations, had largely withdrawn from the St. Lawrence valley by the seventeenth century, driven out and replaced by the Algonquin (Beaulieu and Ouellet in Champlain, 22). Although the often-shifting loyalties and complex alliances among French, English, and numerous native nations of the period make dating difficult, it does appear that during the first half of the eighteenth century in the Lake Erie region and elsewhere, Iroquois were allies of the French (Eccles, *Essays*, 81, 174–75). This may allow a general periodization of setting to a half-century or somewhat more before date of publication.

We are told little about how or where the immigrants live in Canada; there is no mention of a city such as Quebec or Montreal; of church, school, or Jesuit seminary such as those long established there; or of social organization at any level. Saint-Almont abandons the priesthood and becomes tutor to Zoé's son (we hear nothing of other children). They might well live in Montreal or Quebec, where they would be able to enjoy a relatively pleasant and sophisticated urban life, with the husband perhaps in an administrative post befitting his previous colonial experience, perhaps as a wealthy landowning *seigneur* owing fealty to a commercial fur-trading company. Or they might become *habitants*, freehold farmers, perhaps quite prosperous ones. Timon is adopted into an Indian tribe, living and hunting with them in the state of nature to which he has long aspired. Adoption was not uncommon among the northeastern First Nations, especially with captives and the children of enemies; indeed, many *coureurs de bois* (fur hunters and traders) adapted to Indian culture as their best means of survival in the wilderness, and many intermarried. Maréchal's point appears to be that the characters end up free and content, able to make of their lives more or less what they please in a place where nature has not yet been tamed or depleted by commerce.

How would Maréchal have learned about North America and, more especially, about Canada, France's former colony? Reading would be an obvious way. In his personal library of 354 items, catalogued for sale just after his death, we find *La vie de Guillaume Penn, fondateur de la Pennsylvanie* (1791) and *Nouveau voyage dans l'Amérique septentrionale* (1781) by Abbé Robin, among numerous other travel accounts describing the Orient, Europe, and the Americas (Aubert, 156–74). Popular novels might also have been a resource, particularly one by the well-known English writer Frances Brooke, whose novels were frequently translated and republished in France. This was not untypical for the period, which Lorraine McMullen claims "was a period of French Anglomania" (64) during which hundreds of English novels were translated for an enthusiastic French audience. As Harold Wade Streeter points out, thousands of French Protestants had emigrated to England after revocation of the Edict of Nantes in 1685 and the consequent return of official religious intolerance. Many settled in London, where "they constituted themselves the interpreters to Europe of the great controversial English writers" (Streeter, 11), and although these works may not have centered on novels, the project would have created the environment in which a taste for translated novels could thrive. McMullen's observation about anglomania occurs in her study of Frances Brooke, whose best known epistolary work, *The History of Emily Montague* (1769), tells the story of several British colonials living in Quebec, including two young women friends of contrasting personalities. Brooke's detailed portrait of

Canada, and the relationship between the two friends, might well have influenced Maréchal's novella.

A more personal connection was probably the Montréalais Jacques Grasset de Saint-Sauveur, whose five-volume *Encyclopédie des voyages* (1796) was on Maréchal's shelves. This author was also a friend and collaborator. Saint-Sauveur's father was an official in Montreal; the Canadian-born Saint-Sauveur became an artist and engraver in Paris. In that capacity he was one of several illustrators of the magnificent multivolume *Costumes civils actuels de tous les peuples connus* (1788) to which Maréchal provided the text; volume four includes several pages on the Nootka of Canada's west coast, probably derived from Captain James Cook's account of his voyage to the Pacific northwest (see Mannucci, Chap. v). Indeed, he seems a kindred spirit: like Maréchal, he was a prolific writer in varied genres, with a philosophical, political, and erotic bent. Perhaps he related to Maréchal the "très fantastique" (Roy, 2:147) story of Esther Brando or Brandeau, the Jewish girl from Bayonne who, disguised as a Christian boy, spent two years in Quebec until she was discovered and sent back to France in 1739 (see Varin).

Why Canada for this happy ending rather than one of France's Caribbean or South American colonies? In refusing to offer a clear sketch of his characters' lives in Canada (whether under French or British rule) or a clear date for the narrative, Maréchal is able to draw on the quasi-utopian representations of early colonists, explorers, and missionaries such as Lescarbot, Leclercq, and Champlain, whose accounts were frequently reprinted and widely read from the moment of their publication down through the eighteenth century. Closer to his own day, reports from Canada made it clear that in many respects, the settlers were far better off than those working people who remained at home. They enjoyed minimal taxes, free land, none of the violent slums and grinding poverty of major French cities, no feudal remnants under which French peasants suffered until the Revolution ended them, a good social support network of hospitals and charities, little corruption, some democratic institutions (Eccles, *Government*, 13; *Canadian Society*). Thus, the Canadian setting would enable the simpler, more wholesome life for his characters that would have been impossible in a place like Haiti (then known as Saint-Domingue) or any other sugar- or coffee-producing colony worked by African slaves, hence in a condition of severe immorality (as Maréchal would have seen it). Daily displays of horror in the treatment of slaves would have been part of his characters' experience, along with frequent slave revolts, rather than the healthful "natural" life of Canada's natives. As editor of the prominent radical journal *Révolutions de Paris* between 1790 and 1794, Maréchal followed colonial events closely. Indeed, one of his associates at the journal, the admirable Sonthonax, as a colonial administrator in Haiti amidst the constant warfare there, was the first to abolish slavery in his corner of the empire, even before freedom and independence were won from the revolutionary government at home. Moreover, the indigenous Caribbean populations, the Taino and others, had been exterminated earlier on by Spanish colonists, so these territories lacked a substantial population of "noble savages" to adopt Timon or to form alliances with immigrant families. The tropics also, of course, lacked a climate sufficiently similar to that of Europe to permit physical comfort; even the long, snowy Canadian winter, deplored by early writers, was more readily tolerable than suffocating tropical heat.

Is there a political point to the Canadian setting? Perhaps there is, if by sending his characters to a still-French North America Maréchal reminds his audience of what France had lost only a few decades earlier and was still losing. In 1801 and the several years preceding, terrible events were unfolding in France's Caribbean colonies as Toussaint Louverture led black armies in their battles for personal freedom and political independence. Emancipation of slavery in the colonies had been declared by the French National

Assembly in 1794, but there was no easy transition and much resistance from planters, merchants, and conservatives. The fate of these colonies was high on the public agenda during these years both in France and abroad; American landowners in particular feared emancipation as a threat to their own slave system and lucrative slave trade, as did the British in connection with Jamaica. In 1800, Napoleon Bonaparte—now consul and soon to be emperor—began the process, at first legal, then military, of rolling back the achievements and aspirations of Toussaint's revolution. Only near the end of 1803 did the Napoleonic army surrender to the new leader, Jean-Jacques Dessalines, of the country henceforth to be called Haiti. It is an ending Maréchal would have applauded had he survived another few months; perhaps the Canadian ending of his novella is a quiet allusion to the fragility of imperial ambition.

✴ Of course the elephant in the room when discussing this text is the woman question in early revolutionary France. What positions did, and could, women occupy, and what were Maréchal's views on the matter? The issue was central to political discourse and public life of the day. A thorough discussion of the topic is beyond the scope of this Introduction; it has generated an enormous bibliography. Yet it is important to observe that the novella presents a fundamental paradox with respect to this question. On one hand, the heroine displays an adventurous—even ambitious—spirit; she writes eloquently, teaches herself Latin, moves into an apartment of her own before gaining admission to seminary, fulfills her ecclesiastical duties outstandingly well, and succeeds in the rather difficult seminary curriculum well enough to be invited to proceed to full priesthood. On the other hand, she dies a stereotypically melodramatic death, of a "broken heart" (or, as we might say, of anorexia and despair) in a cave, rejecting any opportunity to lead a fulfilling life whether as a single working woman like so many others, or as partner with Timon, or with someone she has not yet met. Her punishment is self-inflicted, true; yet as a consequence of her transgression she suffers and is punished. It will be up to the reader to decide whether these two representations of the heroine contradict one another.

Perhaps most telling in the characterization of Agatha is the contrast with her best friend, Zoé. Not only do their names begin with letters at opposite ends of the alphabet, as a kind of visual reminder of their opposed attitudes and psychologies, but the meanings of these names also, I suggest, play a role in the reader's response. This would be particularly the case for a French reader, for whom the Greco-Latin root of Zoé's name (meaning "life") is a loving literary compliment to Maréchal's wife, an allusion to his beloved, long-lost classical era, and a constant reminder of life itself, hence nature, maternity, and all that promotes and protects life. By the same token, the name *Agatha* (in French, *Agathe*) sounds like the root of the verb *agacer*: to irritate, upset, or provoke. Moreover, Agatha was one of the early Christian virgin saints, martyred because of her religion; it might be said that Maréchal's Agatha is martyred by her religion as well, albeit in a very different way. Interestingly, the breast plays a central role in both stories: the saint's breasts are torn off and then miraculously grow back; the disguised girl is recognized as such when her breast is revealed through torn clothing—a moment commemorated in the single illustration to the novella. Hagiography—a genre with which Maréchal was of course deeply familiar, as a Catholic, a scholar, and a satirist—frequently opens a saint's life with a brief exposition of the meaning of his or her name, so the resonance of a name was ready at hand for Maréchal as a literary device. Lastly, at a time when many novelists used quasi-allegorical names for their characters, based on either meaning or sound, the two young women's names clearly help to produce the moral structure of the novella, a function borne out by the values the young women explicitly embrace in their correspondence. And, since authorial

Saint Agatha with her breasts on a plate, by Francisco de Zurbarán (1598–1664). The painting is owned by the Musée Fabre in Montpellier. (Courtesy Wikimedia.)

choices often have multiple causes, another possible influence might be an English novel, translated in 1797 as *Agatha, ou la religieuse anglaise*. It portrays the conflict of love and religion, but unlike Maréchal's Agatha, the English one is "mistress of herself—of her reason—and triumphed over every propensity not warranted by the strictest duty" (vol. 1, chap. 1, 1).

Zoé constantly exhorts her friend to think things over, to be logical and rational, to accept reality and allow herself to be guided by Zoé's advice and example as a happily married homemaker. "Prudence" is the term often used by and associated with Zoé. She reprimands Agatha for her lack of this virtue, that is, for her imprudence—a characteristic to which Agatha herself admits more than once. For Agatha, on the other hand, the constant theme is her heart, her desire, her "sensitivity." In French, the word is *sensibilité*, and it or its cognates occur several times throughout the story, predicated of Agatha and, in her letters, of Saint-Almont as well. But during the eighteenth century, this word did not have the positive valence that it does today in English, for at the time it was not necessarily a virtue. Rather than indicating perceptivity, keen awareness of others, or even fragility, it denoted a tendency to be unduly excited by or susceptible to physical phenomena and impressions; thus, the word carried overtones of emotionality, even irrationality. We may think of Jane Austen's novel *Sense and Sensibility* (1811) as a fuller and much better known novelistic exploration of the binary represented here by Zoé and Agatha. At the same time, though, Agatha's character is far from simple. Talented and ambitious, resourceful and ruthlessly honest, she is restricted by the values of her culture, even though those values are only partially internalized. Is she a heroine or an anti-heroine? Again, this is the reader's decision.

Agatha is, of course, the fictional female creation of a male author, so it is interesting to observe that he foregoes many of the slanders and insults that some of his contemporaries might have leveled at a woman who dresses as a man—indeed, did level at the occasionally cross-dressing Olympe de Gouges or other women activists regardless of costume. At no time are we encouraged to think of Agatha as someone who is insane, who wants to be a man, who is lesbian, or who is confused about her sexuality; on the contrary, she is portrayed as all woman, all the time. She takes on a man's outfit for specific practical reasons: at first, to explore Paris easily and safely (a serious challenge at the time, as Arlette Farge's meticulous documentation shows); then, to be near her beloved. Unlike the cross-dressed heroine of the thirteenth-century romance *Silence*, Agatha is entirely autonomous: her masquerade is her own decision, not that of parents, and it has nothing to do with inheritance, for she has inherited a comfortable sum from her grandmother. Nor, since she does not have to work for an income, is she in the same situation as the real-life cross-dressers whose stories were told in the press and biographies or autobiographies, so she does not place herself in a dangerous or morally questionable situation. Her project is carefully planned and successfully executed. Indeed, the name she chooses for her life as a seminarian echoes that of her beloved: He is Saint-Almont, she becomes Sainte-Alba, a feminized version. That the names differ only in their last syllables is perhaps emblematic of authorial subversion of the character's intent (*mont* as a height, *ba* pronounced the same as *bas*, or *low*).

What can be said, though, is that paradoxical as Agatha's story may be, the pros and cons just noted do reflect not only Maréchal's attitude toward women but the mainstream attitude of the Revolution itself. Women worked, women led popular uprisings, women wrote, spoke, and demonstrated publicly, including in the National Assembly; they fought in the revolutionary army; yet they were denied full citizenship rights such as the vote and the right to hold public office, attendance at university, and so on. Full enfranchisement was a constant topic for debate over the years, supported by many men as well as women, but the famous "rights of man" were not fully applied to women; indeed, it was only in 1946 that French women won the vote! Those who opposed full citizenship for women did so on the basis of what we would now call an essentialist view of "feminine nature," or of "Nature" herself, who, they thought, had designated women to the honorable roles of motherhood and wifehood, creator and manager of a happy household, teacher to new generations, fighter when necessary to defend the Revolution—but not suited to the rough-and-tumble of active political life. These are attitudes to which Maréchal subscribed. It is, in my view, the underlying problem in the plot of his novella and in the society from which it emanates.

I am reminded here of Fredric Jameson's description of a cultural artifact as "a symbolic act, whereby real social contradictions, insurmountable in their own terms, find a purely formal resolution in the aesthetic realm" (79). A self-willed death and a far-off utopian colony are, in this case, aspects of "aesthetic or narrative form...with the function of inventing imaginary or formal 'solutions' to unresolvable social contradictions" (ibid.). Yet if we return to the text by Claude Lévi-Strauss from which Jameson derived this idea, we find a slightly differently angled perspective, perhaps somewhat less pessimistic. Discussing facial and body decorations in several Brazilian tribes, Lévi-Strauss writes, "On the social level, the remedy [for resolving social contradictions among the Mbaya] was lacking...but it never went completely out of their grasp. It was within them, never objectively formulated, but present as a source of confusion and disquiet. In fact, they dreamed of it... present only in their art, it seemed harmless" (179). There is no mention of unresolvability or insurmountability, and one might infer from Lévi-Strauss's careful formulation that the issue of social resolvability is not absolute but relative, not a human lack but a social one.

✳ For me, the author's retreat from his daring premise doesn't detract from the pleasure of reading his skillfully written novella. What might have been the literary influences? Maréchal's personal library held a recent edition of *L'art épistolaire par Jaufret*, doubtless useful in the composition of an epistolary narrative. We infer, too, that Maréchal admired the epistolary novels of Samuel Richardson, whose name appears in the *Calendrier des républicains* for July 1, along with those of other English writers (e.g., Shakespeare, Milton, and Addison) for other dates. His *Almanach des honnêtes gens* displays a similar anglophilia, with listings for these and others such as Pope, Dryden, Prior, Gay, and Swift, and I have mentioned above the possible influence of Frances Brooke—all or most of these English writers known in translation, to judge by the contents of Maréchal's library.

Another layer of influence can be found, I suggest, in medieval literature. Through his years as a librarian at the compendious Mazarin Library in Paris with its thousands of printed and manuscript volumes (see Molinier),[4] Maréchal had access to a great deal of medieval material. He refers to some of this material in various works, particularly those modeled on, and revising, the traditional almanac or calendar, which would normally feature a saint for each day. Replacing the Catholic saints is a range of early and late medieval figures, both men and women. In the *Almanach des honnêtes gens* we find Héloïse (May 17); she reappears in the *Calendrier des républicains* under the same date. The *Almanach* has Czech reformer Jan Hus (July 16), Petrarch (July 18), the chronicler Jean Froissart (October 7), Abbé Suger (January 13), Mahomet (June 7 and in the *Calendrier*, same date). Dante appears in the *Calendrier* (November 27), as do the philosopher Roger Bacon (September 18) and John Wyclif "martyr" (December 29).

As with the fad for English novels from which Maréchal doubtless benefited, medieval literature was also much in vogue and its traces are visible in his novella. French medievalism emerged in the seventeenth and even sixteenth centuries with concerns about cultural patrimony that arose from civil wars, as well as international "competition for cultural hegemony in Europe" (Zezula, 15); Nathan Edelman adds several further socio-political motives for the development of medieval studies (see especially Chap. 2). The *Roman de la rose* was edited as early as 1526 by the court poet Clément Marot; other editions, collections, and linguistic studies followed, with special interest in chivalry and court spectacle, queens, genealogy, epic, and romance heroes. During the seventeenth and eighteenth centuries, not only creative writers but academicians and scholars debated the meaning of the medieval, as Alicia Montoya shows. And throughout the eighteenth century there was, of course, the "Bibliothèque bleue," the library of paperbound modernized versions of medieval stories peddled around the country by itinerant booksellers; these acquainted much of the rural and urban population with the medieval literary heritage both religious and secular.

Most prominent in popularity was the correspondence between the twelfth-century ecclesiastical lovers and spouses Héloïse and Abelard. Their epistolary story, translated from Latin several times during the seventeenth and eighteenth centuries, generated selections, revisions, and even fabricated new letters (Cizewski, 75). A modern translation found a place in Maréchal's library, and indeed it had influenced one of his heroes, Jean-Jacques Rousseau, for the latter's epistolary tale of a tutor and pupil who, like Abelard and Héloïse, fall in love: *Julie, ou la nouvelle Héloïse* (1761). Maréchal also owned a manuscript Book of Hours, an illustrated Boccaccio, a history of Joan of Arc and another of the fictive Pope Joan (another story of cross-dressing and ecclesiastical success!), several accounts of early French kingship and chivalry, general histories of France, England, Scotland, and other countries including Russia, a biography of Mahomet, histories of the University of Paris (founded in the twelfth century) and the Sorbonne College (thirteenth).

How is this background, both personal and cultural, evident in *La femme abbé*? I've discussed above the influence of hagiography on some of Maréchal's choices in the representation of his protagonist, which are not surprising given his Catholic upbringing and education, as well as his decade-earlier publication of a satirical legendary, the *Nouvelle légende dorée* (1790). But other reminders of the medieval matrix surface throughout, and it is well to remember that, as I've observed elsewhere ("Afterlife," 29–31), the three dominant institutions of the Middle Ages—feudal law, monarchy, and the Catholic Church—lived on even after 1789; the first was finished within a few years, the second in a few decades, the last is still with us. If we read through Maréchal's novella with a medievalist's eye, we spot a number of familiar medieval motifs.

In Letter XVIII, Agatha writes that she is torn between two desires: Zoé's image, like that of a good angel, is at her right, while an evil spirit seems to be at her left. This ancient topos, the *psychomachia* (battle of/for the soul) goes back to early Christian personification allegory. Its later manifestations appear in Romanesque church architecture as well as late medieval and renaissance morality plays, most memorably for English drama in Marlowe's *Faust*. In early French moralities, the prototype is likely the twelfth-century "Jeu d'Adam" with its arguments by Figura (image of God) and Diabolus (Satan) for influence over Adam. Further on in the same letter, Agatha writes that her heart and imagination are allied against her reason. Again, this image of psychic warfare partakes of the allegorical morality-play tradition as well as that of personification allegory best represented in the great thirteenth-century allegory of love, the *Roman de la rose* with its externalized and embodied psychic faculties of both the lover and his lady. In Letter XXI, Agatha notes that most people believe that leisure (*oisivité*) is the cradle of love. Here the allusion is to Oiseuse, an important character in the *Roman de la rose*. Later, in the quarry when Timon offers her a new life in

North America, Agatha replies, "A doe that carries in her flank the spear with which she's been wounded, can go no further." Marie de France's *lai* "Guigemar," probably composed in the late twelfth century, features a mortally wounded speaking doe. (Oddly, this female deer is also a cross-dresser as it were, her head carrying a stag's antlers.) Both Marie and Sylvain might have had in mind an even earlier wounded doe, the one that Dido compares herself to in *Aeneid* 4:69–72, though in both earlier instances the weapon is an arrow, not a spear. In Letter XXII, Agatha justifies her profanation of sacred things by asserting the purity of her intentions; this may allude to the Abelardian theory of intentionalist ethics.

Perhaps most telling of the medieval matrix, though, is the eroticism that Agatha disguises or expresses as religious fervor and on account of which she undertakes her short-lived ecclesiastical career. The nexus can doubtless be traced to late-Jewish and early-medieval allegorization of the explicitly sensual Biblical Song of Songs as a devotional hymn. This exegetical tradition continued down the Middle Ages in religious lyric, sermon, and prayer depicting or addressing Jesus as bridegroom or lover, the Church or the worshiper as bride, suitor, or beloved, and, not least important, the numerous Biblical commentaries by French scholars of the previous two centuries that Maréchal consulted for his own thorough study of Hebrew and Christian scripture, *Pour et contre la Bible*, published the same year as the novella. The writing of French and English medieval women visionaries gives ample attention to this trope. Among writers known for it, whom we know Maréchal read, and whose names appear in his various *almanachs*, we may cite Dante and Petrarch, particularly Dante's *La vita nuova* and Petrarch's *Canzoniere*. Indeed, Agatha implements the programme of much Italian lyric poetry: the beloved as adored saint and source of salvation, Eros as new deity, the practise of erotic desire as pilgrimage or ritual of worship, importuning as prayer, etc. Maréchal had already, in his satirical legendary, expressed the

The Ecstasy of Saint Teresa *by Gian Lorenzo Bernini (1598–1680) is displayed in the Cornaro Chapel, Santa Maria della Vittoria, Rome. The sculptural group portrays Saint Teresa of Avila (1515–1582) with the angel she saw in a vision.*

view that many women become nuns or practise intense lay devotion from non-religious motives, whether to escape the burdens of housework and childbearing, like the blessed Raingarde; to pursue a lesbian friendship (e.g., Saint Guiborat or Saints Sabina and Serapia); to indulge a taste for sadomasochistic "discipline" (Saints Delphire and Elzear, Saint Catherine of Sweden); or to develop an especially close and sexualized relationship with a spiritual advisor, such as that between Jeanne Frémiot de Chantal and her director, Francis de Sales. Maréchal's effort to foreground the erotic subtext of some hagiographical writing is particularly noticeable in his version of the life of Saint Genevieve, patron saint of the city of Paris (Delany, "Saint Genevieve").

Given his broad literary background, and his youthful experience in Parisian salon culture, it is no surprise that Maréchal is able to portray with considerable art and insight the progress of a sheltered young woman's rapid slide into obsession. Though it is clear where his moral convictions ultimately lie, the author refuses to turn his characters—even the doting grandmother, even the unhappy priest—into mere caricatures. Only Zoé, who bears his wife's pet name, remains, as Agatha admits, all good. The author's earlier success as a playwright is surely echoed in the tense emotionality of Agatha's terse dialogues with Saint-Almont, creating suspense as to whether and when she will be discovered. The complex personality of Timon, with whom the author shares opinions and some personal history, emerges with all the contradiction of a real individual, as do the rationalizations Agatha produces to justify herself as a good Catholic despite her real blasphemies, which go well beyond the "imprudence" to which she confesses. I hope that others will enjoy the story as much as I have done.

Translator's Note

OF COURSE the usual question for translators applies: strict fidelity to the original, or liberties taken for the sake of fluency and contemporaneity? With Maréchal, and doubtless many another French eighteenth-century writer, a further issue complicates the decisions: his own stylistic inconsistency, which I noted in my Introduction to *Anti-Saints* and note again here. On one hand, there is the elaborate rhetoric of the period, which Maréchal as a well-educated literary man wants to display, and which his main characters would have some acquaintance with. On the other hand, there is either a satirical intention (as in the legendary) or, for the novella, the rather breathless enthusiasm of a youthful protagonist, who would not realistically correspond with her best friend, or converse with her grandmother, in a consistently elevated style. Underlying everything, to be sure, are the structures of thought represented in the language of the time.

My own tendency is to want to preserve as much as possible of cultural and authorial expression. For the modern anglophone reader it is triply a foreign text: by language, by religious culture, and by period. As a historicist I want to preserve that sense of foreignness. I haven't wanted to remodel Agatha as a phone-toting, North American star-struck stalker (though a limited case could be made for the latter two descriptors). So, for example, I've retained the present tense at places where it occurs, albeit perhaps oddly, in the original, rather than substitute a more usual and fluid narrative past tense; this seems faithful both to the author's desire for dramatic effect and to Agatha's scattered and unreliable mental processes. Similarly, I've retained original punctuation wherever possible, even when our own usage might be slightly different. On the other hand, Agatha addresses or refers to her grandmother with a variety of terms that would make little sense literally translated: "maman," "bonne maman," "ma bonne vieille," "bonne petite maman." I've retained the affectionate tone and variety by using terms familiar to us, such as "grandma" and "granny" in addition to the more formal "grandmother." In other cases I've kept religious and medical terms (e.g., physiognomy, levite, rigorists, etc.) no longer current but that represent middle-class Catholic culture of the era, and trust that my explanatory notes will clarify their significance. In places where a literal translation would sound stilted, I've opted for something more fluid, while at the same time preserving an artfully composed sentence.

The
Woman
Priest

A very brief preface.

This correspondence, written well before 1789, includes nothing supernatural or against nature. The reader, whoever he may be, in closing this book will by no means feel his soul dismayed or afflicted; he'll be done with it, perhaps, for only a few gentle tears.

First letter. Agatha to Zoé. From Paris.

My good Zoé! I won't be able to come tomorrow for your nice invitation. I have a ceremony, a celebration. Guess what kind. A ball? No. An engagement banquet? No. A wedding? Not at all: I'm boring you, you who are so lively, so curious, and so interested in everything that concerns me. All right! I am invited to a first mass. At the very least, I can't get out of accompanying my granny to it. Since she wants almost everything I want, as you know, I sometimes have to do the will of her who replaces my mother. I'll tell you after tomorrow if I was really bored. Luckier than me, you are outside this nasty Paris, breathing the first airs of spring. Goodbye, Zoé.

II

Oh! My very dear friend! How many things I have to tell you! So many that I hardly know where to begin. Listen, or rather read this with as much patience as I have pleasure in writing you this letter.

First, we had to find this first mass at the other end of Paris which is so huge. There were lots of people at this religious celebration, especially a lot of women, and all dressed up. The church was full. This extraordinary gathering made me think. I'm a bit overtaken by something I reproached you about lightly in my first letter. We're all curious! So I asked a few girls my own age about the cause of such unusual zeal for the hero of such a solemnity. A young blonde whispered to me: "The cleric whose first mass you're going to hear is a victim of love. He desperately loved a young woman and believed the feeling was reciprocated. But the unfortunate man was dealing with a flirt unworthy of him, because they say he is a very fine and sensitive man, as is proved by the act of despair that we are about to witness."

These few words interested me very much. I advanced as close as possible to the altar to contemplate the victim and miss nothing of the sacrifice. I found myself in the second row of the women who surrounded the sanctuary. Finally, the procession left the sacristy, to the sound of organs played by Miroir,[1] for they put a lot of elaborate preparation into this occasion, and it was a high mass that was being celebrated by the new priest. He arrives. I see him pass by slowly to reach the first steps of the altar. Dear Zoé! Is it clairvoyance? They say that women are only too susceptible to that, but I never saw, or at least I think I never saw, a face more interesting than that of the young levite.[2] He has, moreover, a fine, well-made physique, to the extent I could observe it under his sacerdotal garb. He lowered his eyes as seemed to be required by the ministry he fulfilled. He didn't walk with a confident step, and it was quite fitting that he genuflected at the first step of the altar. He needed support for his shaky legs. The air of defeat that characterized his whole person was noticed by all those present and inspired the liveliest interest.

The high mass began. At the first *Dominus vobiscum*[3] that he had to utter, a very strange scene occurred as he turned to us all. He raised his eyes a moment and closed them almost immediately, appearing to lose consciousness. The other priests who were assisting approached to support him; one of them came to my side of the altar to ask for a vial [of smelling salts]. Of all the women, I was quickest to offer mine. They made the young levite inhale from it and he regained his senses, but a little noise was heard from the opposite side from where we were. Several people got up; one of them left at the request of her neighbors. The cause of this movement didn't take long to be known. I learned that the flirtatious woman who had inspired a deadly passion in the too-sensitive Saint-Almont (that's what they called the new priest) had come to add insult to injury and to enjoy her triumph. Saint-Almont had recognized the woman, and this unexpected encounter produced the crisis that I have just briefly described to you. My dear Zoé, allow me to terminate my letter here. My trembling fingers refuse to write you anything more about it for the moment.

III   *Agatha to Zoé.*

I didn't finish my story. Saint-Almont continued his mass rather courageously. Toward the middle, one of his colleagues addressed a sort of sermon to him, which I found too short, even though it lasted more than a half-hour, which gave me plenty of leisure to examine Saint-Almont, who was seated in a chair above me at the edge of the sanctuary. He seemed to give all his attention to the speech, which covered the resources offered by religion. "Religion," said the sacred orator, "and especially the priesthood, is a refuge from passions and a port in a shipwreck. What shameful weaknesses it has been able to prevent or correct! Of every type of philosophy, religion is still the most powerful...etc." Saint-Almont listened with eyes closed; frequent sighs painfully escaped his lips. From time to time, he brought both hands to his forehead.

This unfortunate man seemed scarcely to have attained the age required for the priesthood. I would have liked to see and know the woman who was author of his despair, but I managed, after the service, to say a few words to an intimate friend of Saint-Almont. I went up to him in a room next to the sacristy; he was almost as upset as his friend. He said, "Saint-Almont would have made a good citizen; he will be a good priest; whatever his position,[4] he will know how to fulfill its duties like an upright man."

I hazarded a few words: "But he seems resigned to the profession he embraces rather than really convinced that it suits him. The ministry to which he pledges himself, is it really his own choice?"

The retort was: "The upright man is faithful to his commitments, however he may have undertaken them. I vouch for my friend."

Most of those present expected to find Saint-Almont, to congratulate him as is the custom; but he shook off our enthusiasm, and I withdrew, dreamy, with my grandma, who said to me on the way home: "This young man edified me; what did you think of him?" "Very good things. He makes a very fine impression."

Back home, his image followed me into every corner of the house. I went down to our little garden; I didn't even notice the budding flowers that in other springtimes wouldn't have bloomed for me in vain. The adventure of Saint-Almont completely occupied me. I feared the approach of night, and not without a basis. I'll tell you, my good Zoé, I couldn't sleep a wink. Henry IV said, "Paris is well worth a mass."[5] Zoé might reply to me, "That's a lot of trouble for a mass!"

Adieu, my best girl; don't scold me, or at least wait until I come to see you under your pretty lilac-tree arbor. Maybe I'll tell you even more, but not a word to your husband—he'd make fun of me and I'd rather be scolded than mocked. Adieu.

IV Note from Zoé.

Don't fail to come in three days; I'm keeping for then my response to your last letter. Don't fail; arrange to spend a couple of weeks in the bosom of friendship.

V Agatha to Zoé.

Forgive me, my friend, but I can't come to see you so soon. My grandma's health has changed somewhat, and mine isn't the most perfect either, so let's put off the plan. But I can't postpone writing to you, at the risk not of displeasing you but of exposing myself to some small reproaches from you. Really I don't like to pass for better than I am. Mother Nature, in giving me existence, didn't want to make me either prudish or pious, even though since that fatal high mass I haven't missed hearing one every day.

I see you from here laughing secretly. Oh, well! There I am, what can I do? But listen, it was only natural to desire some news of Saint-Almont in his new position. My granny informed me that as regular priest he is limited to the same parish where I saw him start out; consequently I tell her: "Permit me to go hear his second mass. I'm curious to learn whether he has recovered a bit from that crisis he experienced when he ascended the altar for the first time." My granny responded: "Go, my child, follow your good instincts; you were born sensitive and whatever might be said about it, that's to be born fortunate."

So the next day after the first mass, I went to hear a second one. Saint-Almont seemed to have recuperated from his emotion of the previous day. He completed his ministry with dignity. It was at the *Dominus vobiscum* that I examined him to read his physiognomy. I saw there a great sensitivity, and a store of grief that I think time will have great trouble to dissolve.

O my dear Zoé! I have to rely on your indulgence to add what you are going to read now.

Would you believe that I desired to be a man, to have the right to serve the mass to Saint-Almont? I envied the young choirboy who assisted him, the pleasure I imagined this child would have in sprinkling a few drops of water on Saint-Almont's fingers, or in carrying to his lips the hem of Saint-Almont's chasuble. How fortunate he is, I said to myself!

Zoé! Maybe you think I blush in transmitting these details. Not at all! What I feel is doubtless a new type of madness, but at least it isn't a fault. If my spirit is delirious, my agitated heart is not less pure or less worthy of you.

So as to hide nothing from you, know that every day, without once missing, I am going to hear Saint-Almont's mass, which is held at eleven o'clock.

VI *Zoé to Agatha.*

Agatha! You are and always will be dear to me, but you are no longer wise. How in the wink of an eye could he change you to that extent? Agatha enamored of a priest! Where do you think it can go? What is your aim? Lovable and sensitive girl, where are you going to place your first affections? Bad luck has its rights over us. It is fine, it is praiseworthy, it is completely natural to shed a tear for the misfortune of our fellow human beings. But a man who has just raised a wall of eternal separation between himself and women, because he was the plaything of one of them, can he become the object of attachment? But I'm mistaken: my Agatha wanted to amuse herself for a moment, and her intelligence calms me down about her heart. It's fiction that you've written me, right? Agatha will come visit her Zoé, will stay with her for several days; she will continue to be the delight of our social life. If friendship gives me some rights over Agatha, I'll take advantage of them to cure you of this shock to your senses, and you will peacefully await the moment marked by destiny when you will meet the right man to unite with, following my example. Come, my Agatha, enough of make-believe;

be careful, for imagination is sometimes treacherous. The genuine friendship uniting me and you is not. Take its advice. Come, and let yourself be guided for a moment by the hand of your Zoé.

You're right that I haven't communicated your last letters to my husband. Come see us or I'll come looking for you.

VII *Agatha to Zoé.*

Your letter is severe, but I acknowledge its justice. The sentiment that dictated it would be quite capable of curing me, if my malady were not incurable. Yes! Lightning is not faster than what has happened in my heart, and it is all the more wounded because it expected less. You rely on the laws of reason, but what can reason do against the first spark of sympathy? You see, sympathy is not a chimera; you experience it every day in your happy household. That is what unites you to the husband you love. Less fortunate than you, I met the thing I need in a man who can't be mine. Don't blame me; content yourself with pitying me, and allow me to confide in you everything that happens to me. Are we masters of our destiny? If you don't recoil, if you don't disavow me as your friend, I feel I can't be completely unfortunate.

No doubt I love; in vain would I disguise it. But if I confess it to others than myself, it will only ever be to my friend. I will respect myself in her; I will respect her in myself. The sentiment that connects us will preserve me from faults, even if it doesn't preserve me from the grief inherent to a passion admitted by nature but contradicted by social rules.

So don't speak to me about coming to you, and don't come to find me either. Leave me to my illusions; they are such that in wanting to destroy them, one would impute to them a sinister character. Imitate Nature, who is good; be indulgent like her.

Saint-Almont, probably to distract himself from this silent flame that consumes him, commits himself completely to the duties of his position. Apparently he knows that keeping busy is one of the most powerful remedies against love, just as leisure is its most active poison. I see his plan of action; he is wise, and gives me the highest opinion of his judgment. All his days are without a gap; the lectern and the confessional serve in turn as stage for his apostolic zeal. Last Sunday he gave the homily; I was careful not to miss it. I asked a woman who was standing by the church door to let me know when it started. This good woman thought me a saint. "So young, to be already so pious!" she said.

My dear Zoé! If you knew with what grace, with what unction he preaches! The subject of his first speech was love of our fellow human beings. My good grandmama, who wanted to hear him after the account I gave her, and who knows a lot about sermons, squeezed my hand, saying, "My dear daughter! I have followed many preachers in my life; not one of them gave me so much pleasure."

My grandma has never encountered anything like it. Saint-Almont persuades, you only have to see him; he doesn't shout; he doesn't gesticulate like a madman; it's heart speaking to heart.

Something that will astonish you is that he dares to treat love, and even to praise it; but it's because he sees this passion as one of the most beautiful and most sublime in nature. "Love," he said at one point in his homily, "love in a virtuous soul is one more virtue. Happy are those," he added, "happy are those who love one another with innocence!" How beautiful he was in pronouncing this exclamation, which was followed by a long sigh!

I positioned myself in front of him, behind a column; his eyes at that moment shone, sparkled; a lovely blush colored his face. His whole physiognomy was angelic.

My dear Zoé! I say this to you naïvely: what a pity this man didn't meet the right woman for him! How vile she is in my eyes, she who didn't grasp the worth of such a man! A tear falls from my eyes in sharing with you this bitter, useless reflection. I am also irritated with Saint-Almont. Why, being ill-treated the first time, did he give up immediately? Was there only one woman in the world? All the ill we see on earth perhaps only comes from so few people being in their proper place. Goodbye, Zoé; I don't have the courage to write you anything longer. Black grief is carrying me away. You're not in Paris! Indulgent friend, you would save me from myself. Once more, adieu.

VIII *Zoé to Agatha.*

My poor Agatha! Your last letter troubles me. It seems that you enjoy digging a precipice under your feet. Try to interrogate yourself in the calm of reason, and to see yourself coolly. Every day adds to your delirium. You don't see the ills you are preparing for yourself. Instead, imitate the one who is the innocent cause of your straying spirit. See, as you yourself admit, see with what prudence he keeps away from every object capable of calling him back to his unhappy passion. I beg you, don't flatter yourself; it is precisely the purity of your flame that increases its heat. I would fear much less for your peace if you had chosen a subject unworthy of you; that would be only a momentary error. Be afraid of having that error for your whole life. Don't play games with passions. First our playthings, they end by becoming our tyrants. A single serious reflection could suffice to return you to your youthful tranquility. If someone asked me: What do you make of your friend? What is Agatha doing? Tell me, my Agatha, what would I be able to reply? In order to tell the truth, I would have to say: "My friend has fallen in love with a priest."

That alone should make you open your eyes. A priest is no longer a man for a woman. Think about that; don't stay in Paris; run to my arms; that's your place. Give me yourself to watch over; I will render a faithful accounting. You are my treasure; let me be the treasurer! My husband always asks when we will see you, and I am always obliged to lie, telling him, "Her grandma is ill." Ah! It's rather my poor Agatha who is ill, so ill that she doesn't want to get better. Goodbye, naughty girl. What grief I foresee for both of us!

IX *Agatha to Zoé.*

I read your letter three times, wise Zoé; I interrogated myself right away, and my heart responded that it would always be worthy of yours. I may be very unhappy some day, but never capable of causing shame to Zoé. I pronounced that vow; I repeat it every morning on arising, and at night I fall asleep with the sweet confidence that I have not belied my promise.

After this declaration, you must have the indulgence to read the rest of my letter. You will always be my discreet confidante, but never my accomplice, because I will never have a serious fault to reproach myself with. Do you understand, Zoé?

My good granny came to tell me yesterday morning: "Monsieur l'abbé de Saint-Almont will hear confession this afternoon until evening. These meat-eating days[6] he devotes to his ministry. Oh, he will have many penitents, for he is already highly esteemed. So come quickly."

Granny's story excited in me a sentiment unknown to me until then. "He will have many penitents!" I repeated these words with a tone of jealousy. Yes, I'll go right away; I want to know if there are women capable of loving him as selflessly as I do.

So I found myself near the confessional, well before Saint-Almont entered. What reassured me a bit was that I only saw a few elderly women and very young girls. He didn't keep us waiting long. He came in an immaculate surplice. I didn't move away. He patiently heard several elderly women penitents. One of them coming out said to me, "Young lady, this confessor is an angel of gentleness and wise advice. Don't go to any others; you'll be happy with him. I am enchanted with him; I'll send him my two daughters who are your age."

I felt the most violent desire to present myself for confession, to make myself heard and understood to him who of all men inspired in me the most confidence. I don't know what held me back. The importance and singularity of this approach came to mind. Besides, I had promised myself to try nothing without having consulted my friend. Good, wise Zoé! advise me. Do you allow me this new imprudence? For that's how you will doubtless describe the plan I burn to act on. I know how bad you'll find this act forbidden to the irreligious, but it can't result in any serious difficulty; at most, an even stronger esteem for Saint-Almont. Zoé, speak; you are my oracle.

X *Zoé to Agatha.*

Agatha, you seem to consult me with the firm resolution to not execute my orders. Never mind; I will have fulfilled my duty in outlining yours. Do not enter Saint-Almont's confessional; do not add this new wrong to the others. What would you say to him? That you love him? Yes! You are burning to make this avowal to him under the sacred veil of confession. It's a declaration of love that you would offer, imprudent girl! I like to believe in the honesty of Saint-Almont; and I count on yours anyway, even if he were the sort of man to profit from your weakness. But where will all that lead you? I think that the appropriate role for me to play in this business is that of spectator, of confidante at most: sending you back to yourself, appealing to your own heart, if things become more serious. Agatha, then do what you like.

XI *Agatha to Zoé.*

Apparently you regard me as a desperate invalid: you abandon me to myself. I take you at your own words and I hope that we won't have to repent them. Here is what I thought I could permit myself.

Yesterday, I presented myself at Saint-Almont's confessional. There was a crowd. I let the most urgent go by so as to manage a longer conversation, and here it is. My exact and faithful memory will conserve its expressions all my life; I'll do you the favor of leaving out the preliminaries and the consecrated formulas.

AGATHA: My father, the confidence you have already been able to inspire in several mothers with families leads me to you. I am an orphan nineteen years old, whose paternal grandmother took me in and watched over the springtime of my life. I comfort as best I can the winter of her age.

SAINT-ALMONT: What do you wish from my ministry?

AGATHA: How would I dare...

SAINT-ALMONT: My daughter! You are in the season of passions. Might you be experiencing an unhappy one? You would not be the only one exposed to the storms of the heart. It is a tribute one must pay sooner or later.

AGATHA: I am beginning to experience it.

SAINT-ALMONT: Might you be in love?

AGATHA: Alas!

SAINT-ALMONT: For the first time?

AGATHA: Yes, and for the last; for one doesn't love twice, they say.

SAINT-ALMONT: To love is not always a shameful weakness, but too often it is the innocent cause of a great deal of pain.

AGATHA: That's what I fear.

SAINT-ALMONT: Might you be experiencing some obstacles?

AGATHA: Let me open my entire soul to you.

SAINT-ALMONT: Speak.

AGATHA: The situation I find myself in is not typical.

SAINT-ALMONT: Speak, and make use of me if you think that I can contribute anything to your tranquility.

AGATHA: Then know...

SAINT-ALMONT: Your voice is trembling. Be reassured.

AGATHA: Then learn that the one I love is in a profession where he can't reciprocate, even if he were to know that he is loved by me.

SAINT-ALMONT: You surprise me. I don't imagine...

AGATHA: All right, then, know that the man who found the road to my heart, without looking for it, and which he is unaware of, is a priest like you.

SAINT-ALMONT: A priest!

AGATHA: Yes! A priest just like you.

SAINT-ALMONT: How did it happen?

AGATHA: His unhappiness interested me at first, and from pity to love is only a step.

SAINT-ALMONT: And he has no suspicion of the deadly attraction that he has inspired in you?

AGATHA: Not at all.

SAINT-ALMONT: He has never spoken to you?

AGATHA: Never. I don't even know if he has seen me; at least he has not noticed me. His unhappiness and his virtues attracted me to him. When we love, we don't calculate. Perhaps you know this as well as I do? (Saint-Almont did not respond, but he let a sigh escape.) You see, my father, how much I need your good advice. Do you know a remedy for this deadly passion?

SAINT-ALMONT: Did you know the position of the person who inspired it in you?

AGATHA: Yes.

SAINT-ALMONT: He lives in Paris right now?

AGATHA: Yes.

SAINT-ALMONT: But you probably don't try to see him at all?

AGATHA: On the contrary, I have seen him every day without forbidding myself to do so.

SAINT-ALMONT: That's not how you will cure yourself.

AGATHA: I know.

SAINT-ALMONT: Flee—not the danger, there's none to fear—but be very afraid of long-lasting sorrow.

AGATHA: I don't have the courage for that.

SAINT-ALMONT: Your rationality...

AGATHA: My heart...Put yourself in my place.

SAINT-ALMONT: I have only advice to give you.

AGATHA: What do you advise?

SAINT-ALMONT: On your side there have to be sacrifices.

AGATHA: Of what kind?

SAINT-ALMONT: First, give up seeing him.

AGATHA: I don't dare promise that. What evil do I do in seeing him, as long as I don't speak to him?

SAINT-ALMONT: But what do you aspire to in continuing to see him?

AGATHA: I aspire only to the pleasure, surely quite innocent, of loving him without telling him, for I'll die before he knows my secret.

SAINT-ALMONT: You are not the only victim of such an attraction; others too have loved like you at first, and later have shown more courage than you. Strive to imitate them.

AGATHA: That is beyond my strength.

SAINT-ALMONT: I know some who have managed to raise a wall of eternal separation between themselves and the object of their affection.

AGATHA: I congratulate them, but I don't feel that I have sufficient character.

SAINT-ALMONT: Nor I sufficient illumination to guide you. Address yourself to priests more experienced in the holy ministry where I am still a novice.

AGATHA: You refuse me your help?

SAINT-ALMONT: It's that the help I have to give you is inadequate. What do you want from me?

AGATHA: At least some consolation.

SAINT-ALMONT: Let's end this, since I can't succeed in calming you.

AGATHA: I expected more.

SAINT-ALMONT: Count on my prayers, and accept…I am uncomfortable…

AGATHA: Will you permit me to come back in a few days to consult you?

SAINT-ALMONT: It isn't necessary. Your cure is in your power more than in mine.

AGATHA: You are abandoning me.

SAINT-ALMONT: Present yourself to the high penitentiary.[7]

AGATHA: Am I such a great criminal then?

SAINT-ALMONT: You are only to be pitied, and you are not alone on this precipice. I am directing you to an old man full of virtue and experience. Go.

AGATHA: You don't wish to receive me again?

SAINT-ALMONT: If you knew what it costs me to be unable to respond to your confidence—but your confidence will be better placed where I am sending you. May heaven give you its grace!

I wanted to insist, but Saint-Almont closed the little grille through which we had this meeting; and turning to the other side he gave audience to others less troubling for him and less troubled than I.

So I had to leave. It was nighttime, which consoled me for the lack of success of this singular attempt—this bizarre attempt, if you like, my good Zoé. It's that Saint-Almont couldn't see my face, so consequently I conceived the hope of another interview with him. In this scheme, I also took the precaution of disguising my voice.

On reading this letter containing the extract of what happened in Saint-Almont's confessional, you will repeat: "All right! What is your aim, Agatha? If you truly love, model yourself on the object of your love. Be just as wise, just as reserved, as he is." And I will reply that the more I know Saint-Almont, the more I find reasons to love him even more; and assuredly as long as things don't go further, there is not the least reproach to make against me.

But you're going to protest another project I'm turning over in my mind! You'll think I turned away from it completely, and you'll be wrong again. So know that, without any further circumlocution, I've resolved to dress like a man in order to see Saint-Almont more often and more comfortably. Without explaining my motive, I've already discussed this plan with my grandma. She didn't have the courage to forbid me, so when I receive your response to this letter I will proceed to doing it. Your Agatha is giving up the clothing of her sex, without abandoning its modest virtues. I repeat, I intend to keep myself worthy of your friendship and of my self-respect. Adieu; I embrace you, and ask you to make peace for me with your husband, if he should be in the mood to scold me. Adieu, my good girl.

XII *Zoé to her poor Agatha.*

My poor and always dear Agatha! Are you crazy? Really! You want to renounce your sex: this is all you needed! But tell me, have you reflected seriously on the consequences of what you're allowing yourself to do and with a frivolity that is beyond me? Come back to yourself; remain my Agatha. Remain that lovable, clever girl, interesting and cheerful. Have mercy! Retrace your steps and be afraid of losing yourself. See the road you've already raced down in such a short time; at least, above all, come see us for just one day. If you refuse us this time, you will upset us more than you think. Give to friendship at least the lucid intervals that love leaves to you. Benefit from them. Continue to be our friend. Perhaps Zoé deserves the sacrifice of a few hours of your time. No more from Zoé for Agatha, if you persist in not seeing me!

XIII *Agatha to her Zoé.*

Your letter arrived this time only two days after its date. I couldn't endure this delay or waiting for your news in order to do what I have to announce to you. Yesterday morning, I appeared in men's clothing before my grandma, at lunchtime. She didn't recognize me at first, but I threw myself into her arms, saying, "What! You don't recognize your own granddaughter Agatha?" At the sound of my voice, tears of pleasure flowed from her eyes; she said, "You are a trickster! I already loved you so much; did I need this pretty disguise to love you still more? This suit becomes you! It gives you a saucy air that I just adore."

"My good granny, since I don't displease you in this outfit, would you allow me to wear it often? I'll only be more disposed to help you; this outfit, more convenient than the other, will even let me be more useful to you than in the past. From now on I'm going to try to go out in these clothes and to take a long walk. I'll go as far as the neighborhood where you took me to mass several months ago."

"Go, my child," said my granny, "and be careful of accidents; I would be inconsolable."

So I went right away, with the speed of a bird, to the church served by Saint-Almont, and I arrived at precisely the moment when he left the sacristy to ascend the altar. I offered to assist him during the mass. The choirboy couldn't ask for anything better. You had to see me walk in front of Saint-Almont! Under an expression of remorse I hid as best I could the contentment I felt.

At the chapel, I acquitted myself of my duty fairly competently. I had taken care several days beforehand to study the technique of serving a priest at the altar.

Nonetheless my whole body trembled; my knees bent under me. When it came to the *lavabo*,[8] Saint-Almont, who noticed my distress, deigned to say in the middle of his prayer, "Young man! Be reassured." I answered him with lowered eyes, "This is the first time I've performed this service; I'll do better at the next mass."

Oh, my Zoé! You can't imagine the pure pleasure I savored. Rigorists will consider me a sacrilegious person: they will be wrong. It isn't to mock sacred things that I acted thus; I only wanted to see up close a man whom I esteem above all others and whom I love with the most perfect selflessness. There is nothing in that to blame me for: I am more to be looked at with pity or amusement. Could I offend a good God in showing myself driven, anxious to serve the wisest of the ministers of his altars? Oh, how edifying is Saint-Almont, how affecting his piety, how he would have loved a woman who reciprocated! He has all the tenderness of a lover, and all the candor, all the simplicity, all the innocence of a child. I am very sure that in the person of the young man who helped him at mass he was far from suspecting the young orphan of nineteen who presented herself a few days earlier at his confessional. At the elevation of the host, I kissed the hem of his chasuble more than thirty times; the normal custom is to touch it only once with one's lips. At the end of the mass, the celebrant gives his benediction to the people; I dared to lift my eyes furtively to Saint-Almont at that moment. He appeared to me like a divinity full of sweetness and indulgence. Never had he made such an impression on me; his eyes said a thousand things that went right to my soul. Ah, if only the benediction he gave could pour into my heart the calm that already seems re-established in his!

Saint-Almont seems born fortunate. He never experienced those strong passions, like shocks, that can shake you and knock you over. Ah, had he only met someone better! But whatever may happen to him, he will be able to compensate for his lack of happiness with the comfort of a steadfast peace of mind. If only I had his character!

I joined with all my heart in the actions of grace that he spoke of on returning to the sacristy, where I intended to lead him. Some good women, as we passed, said to one another, "How well this young man served the mass! What zeal he put into it! You don't see many like him any more."

Saint-Almont thanked me with an affectionate air, and I went to take my place in the church, after he had left the altar, to catch another glimpse of him when he returned to his lodging. Kneeling at the base of a pew, I procured this innocent satisfaction, which could appear neither affected nor suspicious. Then I went home, full of his image. The rest of the day was one of the sweetest times of my life.

What will you think of me, my Zoé? I've told you everything; my soul is naked before you. What reassures me is that this episode causes me no remorse at all. When I do something bad, my conscience doesn't let me ignore it. Zoé won't be more severe than my own conscience, will she? Adieu.

XIV *Agatha to Zoé.*

You haven't replied to my last letter; that's a shame. I prefer your reproaches to your silence. Write me; don't spare me, please; say whatever is in your heart, but write.

I won't imitate you, at least in that. I'm going to send you another letter, to tell you that I've continued my little exercise. Every day I serve Saint-Almont's mass. You are the only one, Zoé, who is not edified: everyone refers to me as a prodigy of piety. Saint-Almont himself has noticed my assiduousness and has said a few flattering words to me about it. These few words have spread balm on my wound. Yes, I want to continue to love him this way; we risk nothing, neither he nor I. Besides, he is as much a stranger to my love as to you whom he has never seen. So I am happy to love him, although without hope: I love only for the pleasure of loving. This enjoyment[9] is doubtless permitted. Who can find anything in it to reproach? Whom do I wrong? Once more: is there anything wrong in assiduously attending all the offices of the church, placing myself in the choir in the stalls below his, and furtively giving myself the pleasure of seeing him, of hearing him chant? He has such a lovely voice! The most beautiful tune of Sacchini[10] at the Opera is not worth an *oremus*[11] from Saint-Almont's mouth. This morning, he performed the aspersion;[12] I didn't lose a drop. Repeating the sign of the cross, I gathered on my fingers the water that landed on my forehead, and brought it to my lips. Tonight it will bring salvation; I'll go to breathe the incense he will offer on the altar.

Meanwhile, carnival[13] is coming. What pure enjoyment I promise myself! While other women run to the dances, I will attend the forty-hour prayers; I will be seen, not far from the prie-dieu where Saint-Almont will take his place, intoxicated with the pleasure of contemplating him at leisure. He is far from understanding what is going on around him. No matter; I want to love him as one loves God, without knowing whether God deigns to take any notice of the homage paid him by weak mortals.

Adieu, my dear Mentor-Zoé.[14]

XV *Zoé to Agatha.*

My dear, misfortunate Agatha! I'm going to inform you of news which I'm only too certain will give you less pain than it does me. I was becoming a preacheress who would have ended by seeming annoying to you. Reassure yourself: now you are free from my sermons, much to my regret, for I can't stop loving and pitying you. However, I have to tell you that my husband, who wanted so much to travel, has obtained a pretty good position in one of our colonies far across the sea, and we have to leave right away. I won't have time to await your response to this letter; the Minister of the Navy is urging our departure. Ten thousand miles away from my Agatha I will still write her; but what delays and misfortunes my letters will undergo! If only I'd been able to dissuade my husband! Your fate, my very good friend, truly alarms me. I leave you to your own mercy, without advice, without a friend. Swear, in the depth of your beautiful soul, to think of your Zoé, and of all the promises you have made her. Adieu; I embrace you with an anguished heart. When will we receive each other's news? When will we see each other again? In my first letter I'll hope to be able to designate the place where you can address your cherished letter. Ah! My friend! Only three days to wait, and I would love to take you with us whether you wanted to or not. Adieu, my soul's other half.

XVI *Agatha to Zoé.*

Zoé! You don't know your friend. Do my faults give you the right to be unjust toward me and to affront our friendship? Am I reduced by them to letting you know that your last letter struck me to the heart? In reading it, I felt abandoned by the whole earth. Zoé! My friend! Wise Zoé, who was my Providence, my refuge, now sails beyond the sea; that was the most sinister thing that could happen to me. I won't reply to your sarcasms; rather, to make you repent them, here's what I imagine. Zoé, transplanted beyond the sea, will be no less present to my mind; I shall continue to write to her as if she were still in her countryside. My illusion will be far from complete, since I won't receive your news any longer. No matter; I will make it my duty to consult you in the future just as in the past. You will be my second conscience. From tonight on, I am starting a journal of my life, and it will be addressed to you. I will tell you my mistakes, I will recall your advice, and God will do the rest. This is the best I can imagine to convince you of both my attachment and the importance I place on your esteem and friendship. I like to think that we will see each other again; you will find me still worthy of calling myself the friend of Zoé's heart.

XVII *Agatha to Zoé.*

Ah! My friend! Everything is abandoning me all at once: one abyss calls forth another. Scarcely do I learn of your departure for the islands, and of our separation, than I have to absorb another loss. My wonderful granny has just succumbed to the infirmities inseparable from advanced old age. How her last moments touched me! She gave up her last sigh in my arms, but she had the time, as they say, to see herself die and to die with all the aids of religion. Feeling herself more and more enfeebled, "My good little Agatha," she said in a changed voice, "do something for me; it will be the last time, I think, but not the least. Do you think that the worthy ecclesiastic whose first mass we heard with so much edification would grant me the favor of administering [the last rites] to me? Go find him; he noticed you for your constant piety; perhaps he won't refuse you."

My dear Zoé! I'm sure you don't doubt my hurry. I flew immediately in my men's clothing to Saint-Almont's presbytery. I climbed up to his apartment with some confidence. This meeting wasn't about me; nonetheless I was far from indifferent in this effort. Saint-Almont didn't refuse me. He stopped his work to accompany me without displaying the least ill humor at my insistence. However, I thought I noticed that he was in the heat of composing a speech that he had to give. I poured out excuses and gestures of supplication. "We owe ourselves," he said, "to all men and women who claim our assistance." During the walk back, he maintained a silence that I didn't dare break; but I compensated for that by looking at him cautiously (for fear of embarrassing him), for he is shy and modest, as a good quality and a virtue. At my grandma's bedside it wasn't possible for him to converse with her. He got from her only some signs of satisfaction. His presence, although mute, was a benefit for which I thanked him with tears in my eyes and squeezing his hands in mine. He pulled them back rather abruptly, and left.

Ah! Zoé! I promised to accuse myself of all my faults to you; you are and always will be my director.[15] So shall I tell you about it? The presence of Saint-Almont diminished for me the sentiment of loss of my grandma, and softened in my heart the horrors of her death.

Evenings and nights, left to myself, I found myself as if alone in a desert. No more friend, no more mother, now I am truly an orphan; and need I cap off my misfortune by carrying in my heart an unhappy and sterile passion?

I can't close my eyes. What will I become? I'm overwhelmed by a thousand thoughts, while a distant relative, whom I warned, was willing to take on all the sad details which accompany and follow an event like the one whose victim I was. Ah! Zoé! From where you are now, inspire your unfortunate and too sensitive Agatha.

XVIII   *Agatha to Zoé.*

Wise Zoé! You who are reason itself, prudence itself, what will you say some day about me? And what's the use of evoking your spirit, of recalling your advice, if I profit so poorly from them? But shall I tell you? An evil genie seems to be at my left, while your image, like that of a good angel, is present at my right, for every decision I take. Here's something strange, but it's stronger than me; love doesn't excuse everything, but it finds nothing difficult, nothing unusual; everything seems natural to it as long as it satisfies itself. Zoé! you are impatient to know where this whole preamble will lead us. Here it is.

For several months now, I have no longer stopped wearing my men's clothes—I was authorized in that by several examples. Abbé de Saint-Almont, who saw me every day behind him in his church, suspected nothing about my disguise. He might have been able to learn the solution to the mystery when he was called to my dying grandma's bedside, but she was beyond speaking to him so she couldn't propose what she had already suggested to me: that he should be the spiritual director of her granddaughter Agatha. That's how my secret was kept. In my neighborhood, a few people know who I am; but at the other end of Paris in Saint-Almont's parish, they are completely ignorant of me. My grandma, feeling herself near the end, used her last moments to hand over to me a considerable deposit of gold money, to which she planned to add a supplement. The distant relative who'd been called to spare me the confusion of the disagreeable circumstance I was in went back to the countryside where he lived. So I found myself mistress of my person and of the small sum left at my disposal. You'll guess my first step, clairvoyant Zoé. I don't need to tell you that I quickly moved my household things to the neighborhood of Saint-Almont's presbytery; I moved into the most modest residence I could find; I turned without constraint to all the practices of piety while maintaining (I do myself this justice) the modesty of my sex, of which I have forsworn only the costume. For several months, I found myself nearly happy. At almost any time of day I could intoxicate myself with seeing my lover without remorse, and didn't worry that my assiduity was taken badly. I had placed my love under the safeguard of religion. This state of affairs should have satisfied me. By no means: my heart and my imagination allied against my reason, so here I am giving birth to the boldest, most bizarre project that any twenty-year-old girl has ever dared conceive.....But this is enough to tell you in one letter. The next one will probably announce the strangest change of circumstance for a woman, and my style will echo the seriousness of my new profession. Ah! Zoé! What love makes us do!

XIX *Agatha to Zoé.*

My affectionate friend! Perhaps you will never read these pages I write you today; or, if you read them, there will be no more time for me. Alas! I put myself in your place and I pity myself; but apparently my destiny must be accomplished. Hear me, you who are my invisible guiding angel. But no, it's no joke; I will never permit myself to joke about the religion into which I was born; and

I require all the purity of my intention so that we won't be frightened—especially me—by the role I propose to play. However, let's reason together for a moment, my good and too wise Zoé. Holy things are not completely forbidden to women, but the condition of being a nun is no less frightening or worthy than the one I have just embraced. In a word, my dear, your Agatha has entered the seminary. "The seminary, good God!" you will cry; "but are you mad? Oh, my Agatha!...do you appreciate all the consequences of such a path? A girl of twenty a seminarian!...."

Why not, severe Zoé! Is a girl seminarian a stranger figure than a girl novice with the Carmelites or elsewhere?

"After this," you'll add, "Agatha is capable of anything. Great God!"

Just a moment, my dear Zoé. Remember that I promised solemnly, and in writing, that I would never permit myself anything contrary to virtue. And moreover, I ask: do you believe me capable of everything just because changing sex on the outside, I am entering a seminary to be closer to the man I love in all the purity of my soul?

But as a favor, read to the end and hear the outcome of all this before condemning me. Pay attention.

I learn that Saint-Almont is so well esteemed that they are giving him an establishment considered both delicate and important in the church. He's been named superior at the seminary. This news strikes my spirit with a sudden gleam. I say to myself immediately: Saint-Almont thinks I am a young man and is favorably disposed toward me. He has no doubts about me; on the contrary, he has noticed the pious character I maintain around him. What problem would there be in presenting myself to be received among the young clerics who live under his discipline? For several years now, religious fervor has noticeably cooled. People such as I appear to be are beginning to become rare. The sanctuary needs exemplary ministers to set right the scandals that multiply day after day. No doubt I will be accepted; and I will have as mentor, as director, as teacher the only man who is dear to me. I will dwell, I will live under the same roof, and I will savor the innocent enjoyment of seeing and hearing at every moment the one I bear in my soul: and all that without compromising myself. I will supervise myself with care; I will neglect no precaution to render the illusion complete, and at least I will be as happy as I am allowed to be, without betraying my duties, without compromising my sex, and whatever she may say, always worthy of my Zoé. I leave the rest until tomorrow evening.

XX *Agatha to Zoé. From the seminary.*

Zoé! Scold me now; but what you will call at the very least a noteworthy folly is done: your Agatha is at the seminary. Here she is, a cleric; but I have to give you the details.

So I get to the door of the seminary; I ring the entry bell; I ask to speak to Monsieur the superior; I am admitted into his rooms. He wasn't alone; I hesitate, addressing him with my first words; I stammer them. My timidity is noted, he guesses that I wish to be alone with him. The three young ecclesiastics—whom he was probably instructing—withdraw, saluting him with respect mingled with affection. Here is my dialogue.

SAINT-ALMONT: Good young man! What do you wish of me?
AGATHA: Sir (I say in a trembling voice), do you recognize me?
SAINT-ALMONT: If I'm not deceived, you are the person who for some time has been very assiduous in the holy offices at the parish church where I first performed the ministry of the altar.
AGATHA: I am the same person.
SAINT-ALMONT: What have you to say to me?
AGATHA: I come to obtain from you the favor of entry into the seminary that you direct.
SAINT-ALMONT: Who are you, good young man?

AGATHA: An orphan, who has just lost his only relative in Paris and who has absolutely no idea where he should find the rest of his family. Alone and as if abandoned in a great city that I don't know well, I come here guided by attraction as well as by the fear of remaining much longer in society. Here is a purse of three hundred louis;[16] it's my entire fortune, please deign to be its depositary.

SAINT-ALMONT: Keep this money. So you have no one here whom you might ask for a reference?

AGATHA: I had a childhood friend who left me only to set up a household. I have lost her; she is now at sea with her husband; only she and the relative whose death I mourn could testify for me and my conduct…But yourself… Monsieur…

SAINT-ALMONT: I can attest your pious perseverance over the past year. What is your plan?

AGATHA: You have just heard it: to be accepted into this seminary and to start studying, under your supervision, for the priesthood.

SAINT-ALMONT: It's a very serious enterprise.

AGATHA: I know.

SAINT-ALMONT: Have you fully developed this resolution?

AGATHA: Yes, sir, and your virtues have determined me. I want to attach myself to you; serve me as father, tutor, guide…

SAINT-ALMONT: You are at the age of passions…

AGATHA: I feel only one of them.

SAINT-ALMONT: Speak, good young man.

AGATHA: That of imitating you.

SAINT-ALMONT: Have you done some studying?

AGATHA: For several months I've applied myself with all the ardor I'm capable of, and I know enough Latin to understand our sacred scriptures. God and you will do the rest.

SAINT-ALMONT: Good young man, I can admit you into this establishment only on a trial basis.

AGATHA: I desire no more; I hope that you will find in me the talent to imitate your virtues. Alas! Don't reject me: a fragile plant, abandoned alone to every wind, I need a tutor and a shelter.

SAINT-ALMONT: You must already grasp that the life one leads in a seminary is laborious, austere...

AGATHA: I know; but your good example will make it easy for me. I swear to you that, without the reputation of your merit, I would never have dared aspire to a place here; I owe you my salvation.

SAINT-ALMONT: Come back in three days.

AGATHA: Three days is a very long time...

SAINT-ALMONT: In three days.

    They seemed like three centuries. Still, they were necessary for me to prepare myself for the new role that I did not fear to take on. I relied a lot on love; it's a god who also makes miracles. Nonetheless, I reflected a lot; I knew how indiscreet and reckless love is, and I needed the greatest circumspection to conceal two secrets at once: my heart and my sex. Oh, my good Zoé! You have never been through such trials; you loved without contradiction and you possess with no troubles the sweetest, gentlest man. I'm happy for your happiness; sympathize in turn with the troubles I endure, and pardon my imprudence. Adieu.

    P.S. You saw on me the most beautiful head of hair in the world; I have just sacrificed it, effortlessly, to my lover, who is now my superior. I cut the hair myself into a round shape. How many women would have wetted it with tears before bringing the scissors near! This natural luxuriance cost me no regret. My only ornament is my love.

XXI *Agatha to Zoé.*

From afar as from near, I am certain that the wise and good Zoé thinks of her poor, mad Agatha; as I do of her: this journal bears witness to that.

So here is Agatha installed in the seminary. Seminary life is not quite as rough as I had imagined at first. The exercises of piety and hours of study are frequent, it's true; but as everything is on a schedule, the task seems less difficult.

But I notice that what is considered truth does undergo occasional exceptions. For example, one is taught to believe that leisure is the cradle of love and that its contrary, assiduous and persistent labor, expels that passion. I experience here quite the opposite. My endless busyness only sustains my love. It's true that I am almost always under the eyes of the one to whom I have vowed my existence and all my faculties. How attentive I am to the lessons he gives us! He gives them to us so affectionately! Persuasion, even more than conviction, makes us adopt all the religious principles he professes. Under such a teacher, I am vain enough to believe that I will make progress in a study so infrequently within the reach of women.

It's been ten days since I joined the seminary; it seems like ten minutes. Emboldened by the encouragement that Saint-Almont has given me, I took the chance of asking him (when I was accompanying him back to his apartment door) if he was happy with me, and what time limit he placed on the type of novitiate he had recommended for me. "Good young man," (he continues to call me this, and this expression that he uses only for me flatters me infinitely), "good young man," he replied, "wait until the end of a fortnight; I think we will be satisfied with one another."

These words give me courage beyond my sex.

And these details, my good Zoé, will prove to you how innocent is the stratagem that I employ to enjoy the presence of him whom I love with a selflessness that is certainly quite rare. Do agree, my friend.

XXII *Agatha to Zoé.*

The fortnight over, Saint-Almont bid me enter his rooms; it was to tell me that he believed me capable of the vocation indispensable to the condition I wanted to embrace, and that he received me willingly among his neophytes.

I thanked him for this grace in the most expressive terms and I seized the occasion to beg him to be the treasurer of my little treasure. He thought for a moment and consented. So there it is: my little fortune and all my being are in the hands of the man I love.

The seminarians I live with aren't numerous, and I don't socialize with any one of them in particular, despite the advances of several. I repel them with constant assiduity in my duties, and with a certain reserve that seems not to displease our superior.

The head of these types of establishment normally chooses from the ecclesiastics he governs the one among them whom he's most pleased with, to be his clerk; that is, his private secretary; and this is a favor which can only be much sought after. This kind of position confers certain privileges: you accompany the superior everywhere, you live near him. It also exempts you from certain common exercises.

All my ambition was one day to become the fortunate being that Saint-Almont would choose when he'd no longer have the one I saw with him when I first entered. This was a very wise young man, belonging to a distinguished family. Two months after my admission to seminary, I learned that his family had obtained for him a benefice which did not entail the care of souls; I redoubled my zeal and piety so as to replace him next to Saint-Almont.

My God! Pardon me if I have dared to make sacred things serve a profane love; but it is you who have put passion into our hearts; they are not crimes—I feel this in the purity of my intentions.

XXIII *Agatha to Zoé.*

Oh, how even the purest, most disinterested love causes torment and worry! It is never satisfied. I live under the same roof as Saint-Almont; I take his lessons; I eat at the same refectory; I wake up and go to bed at the same time as he does, and yet I am still not content. This position as secretary that I crave deprives me of sleep from fear of being unable to succeed. I am not the only cleric he seems to like. There is another he seems to be fond of too, and perhaps that one will obtain the position I am ambitious for. If I fail, I believe I'll fall sick over it.

All these ideas, piling up in my brain, make me imagine a bold stroke that could succeed for me. It is to ask to fill the place of private clerk to Saint-Almont. Would this annoy him? No matter! My impatient spirit can no longer restrain itself. Ah! Zoé! Zoé! France, they vulgarly say, is the paradise of women. Alas! I find there only my purgatory.

XXIV *Agatha to Zoé.*

That's how I like to entitle each page of my journal. This title creates a pleasant illusion for me. I seems that I'm really writing you a letter, and that you'll read it soon. I need to believe that you're nearby and able to watch over me. Alas! You exist for me only in the memories of my heart; wide seas separate us, perhaps forever. Perhaps I won't exist any more when you return to the continent and to our homeland.

One night, after group prayer, I asked, trembling, whether Saint-Almont would permit me to address a few words to him in private. He accepted my wish; I entered with him into his little oratory and said:

> AGATHA: My most honored superior, we have learned that your secretary is leaving the establishment.

SAINT-ALMONT: Yes, I'll be sorry to lose that young man. He's an excellent person.

AGATHA: We all love him.

SAINT-ALMONT: So, my dear Sainte-Alba... (This is the name I use in the seminary.)

AGATHA: Dare I ask whether you have already made your choice to replace him?

SAINT-ALMONT: Not yet, not exactly.

AGATHA: You will no doubt choose the most deserving, alas!

SAINT-ALMONT: Why alas?

AGATHA: It's because more than any of the young ecclesiastics who live here in this seminary, under your peaceful and wise discipline, I would need to be continually under your supervision...Poor orphan that I am...you are my most honored superior, you would be like my father, my tutor, my guardian angel. I would measure my every step by yours. I must reveal my soul to you completely. Know that I couldn't live away from you; it's only your merits that have determined my vocation. Allow me to attach myself to your person and to accept near you all the services it will please you to entrust to me. Don't do me the injury of believing that in speaking to you thus, in coveting this position, I am thinking of the little privileges attached to it; I mean on the contrary to redouble my zeal and labor. That's all: I desire ardently to be your clerk. You will help me to combat passions, to conquer them. Pardon, my most honored superior.

SAINT-ALMONT: Good Sainte-Alba! You haven't offended me, and my trust will correspond to the candor of your sentiments. Go in peace, and continue as you have done up to now.

These last expressions calmed me considerably; I passed a pleasant and nearly happy night. Two days later, our superior's clerk bid farewell to his co-disciples and left. The third day, Saint-Almont called me into his office and had me sit at a desk, saying, "Fulfill with me the functions you have seemed to desire; I hope we will both be content."

Zoé! You can't share the happiness of your Agatha. Here I am, the secretary, friend and almost confidant of the man I love, who is so worthy, through his misfortunes and his virtues, of the attachment of an honest and sensitive heart. We have become almost inseparable; we are separated only at night. I accompany him every place, all the time. Pure felicity, such as the angels must taste in heaven!

XXV *Agatha to Zoé.*

I must tell you, my dear Zoé, that Saint-Almont and I have become the edification of all who see us. When skeptics pour out their sarcasm about the ecclesiastical condition, people answer: "They'd have another opinion if they knew Saint-Almont and his young clerk Sainte-Alba."

During festival rites, they single us out. "What heartfelt piety," they exclaim! "No hypocrisy there. The way this young clerk has his eyes constantly raised to his superior!"

If everyone knew the real motive that makes me behave this way…Well, it's been said before me, and perhaps I am the only one to experience it: "Yes! Love is virtue in a virtuous heart."

I have to serve my lover at the altar at the morning and evening services. You ought to see me as I amorously press against my burning lips the paten[17] that Saint-Almont gives me saying "*Pax tibi*," and I kiss it three times rather than one, on the spot where he kissed it first. As for the *pax tibi*, alas! The religious wish he addresses to me is far from my heart; peace is banished from it for a long time, I think.

At vespers, during the *Magnificat*, you know, my Zoé, that the clerk censes the celebrant; instead of three swings of the censer,

I often give six or nine. They've had to warn me about my error and I blushed to the whites of my eyes. But what satisfaction I experience in publicly offering pure incense to the special man, the only man I will love in my entire life!

At the introductory rites, I am one of the two clerics who, walking a little behind, cense the holy sacrament—what is called the sun—carried by our superior. Sacrilegious that I am, alas! it isn't to God that I direct the incense I burn at this moment. It's completely for Saint-Almont alone.

Sometimes, to give young ecclesiastics practice in the holy ministry and to instruct the people, Saint-Almont sets up edifying demonstrations at church in the evening. I helped him with one; it centered on profane love. Saint-Almont played the role of Our Lord, as suited him, and I the role of the world. To speak plainly, he was the advocate of the good God and I of the devil. Saint-Almont is considered very eloquent. But this time, the whole audience agreed that the pupil spoke better than the teacher. They went so far as to say that the clerk embarrassed his superior in more than one place.

Returning to the seminary, Saint-Almont broached something with me about it, not that he was tainted by low jealousy, but as a wise man, he made me understand that I had reason to fear one day, sooner or later, the arousal of the most terrible of passions. "What have I to fear," I replied, "if you don't withdraw your preserving hand from me?" I added: "Have I not promised to accompany you as a shadow follows its body? And I willingly renew, in all the sincerity of my soul, this sacred engagement."

What is love? How everything it sees is ennobled and becomes interesting!

Would you believe, Zoé, that I experienced a pleasure equal to what they call voluptuousness when Saint-Almont, on Ash Wednesday, traced on my forehead with his thumb a cross in consecrated ash? I could hardly manage to put my hood on my head for fear of erasing from my forehead the fingerprint of my lover.

During Lent, the more frequent confession embarrassed me very much. Fortunately Saint-Almont is as ignorant as I am about love. Besides, he is so far from suspecting the mystery!

On Palm Sunday, a new scene. At mass, we are reading one of the four Passions of Jesus; and toward the end of this reading, the celebrant and all the assistants simultaneously kiss the ground. I waited until Saint-Almont had accomplished this holy duty and then placed my mouth precisely at the place still marked by his breath.

My Zoé, I seem to hear you saying, "Poor Agatha, you're crazy enough for a straitjacket!" That may be, but admit that my madness is more innocent than the affected reason of certain women.

Holy Thursday I permitted myself something even more strange; I can't keep anything hidden from my best friend. This day is consecrated to the priestly[18] Easter. I had to take communion with the others, but it was from the hand of my dear Saint-Almont. Imagine, Zoé, what went through my head—imagine! Not everyone would be as indulgent as you, when you find out. They would consider this action as a horrible profanation. I adroitly withdrew the holy wafer from my mouth, because it had passed between Saint-Almont's two fingers; I conserve it as something precious, and I bestow on it innumerable tender kisses.

The evening of this holy day, our superior publicly washed the feet of the youngest seminarians, and I was among them. Never in my life did I experience an emotion more delicious. Oh, love, love!

The next day we all went to the adoration of the cross; it was held leaning between the arms of Saint-Almont. Ingrate! It's you I was adoring, it's only to you that I addressed those marks of love and piety which edified so many good souls, dupes of appearances.

Oh, my God! How I would be punished, with what indignation they would chase me out of this seminary if anyone happened to discover these sacrilegious confessions, destined only for my best friend! Oh, my friend! Why have you crossed the sea? Come back quickly. Perhaps there's still time for it—but no! the illness is incurable, it is at its peak, and I fear being unable to resist it much longer.

XXVI *Agatha to Zoé.*

But here is another crisis. The moment has come for me to enter what they call "orders." I've already received the ones called "minor," but the good Saint-Almont believes me worthy of being elevated to the subdiaconate, then to arrive quite soon at full priesthood. I humble myself often; I strongly dispraise myself, purposely to avoid accepting this serious commitment, which moreover would make me leave the seminary, where I'd like to remain forever, at least as long as Saint-Almont is there. What to do? Who will give me advice? Zoé, from where you are, send me some wise inspiration; but I wait in vain and I can't ask for a delay; Saint-Almont is urging me. What to decide?

XXVII *Agatha to Zoé.*

Oh, my Zoé! Pity me, don't deprive me of your respect. It's done, this letter is doubtless the last I will write you. If it ever arrives at its address, Agatha will no longer exist for her Zoé, nor for anyone else; neither you nor Saint-Almont will ever hear me spoken of again. Adieu forever.

Here is what happened. The seminary where I am (or where at least I was then) owns a country house a little way from Paris. It's a delightful retreat, and the seminarians, in good weather, go there for recreation at least once a week, under the superior's watch. We went there toward the end of May, between Easter and Pentecost. Scarcely had we recovered from the walk than Saint-Almont took me aside in a thick, flowery copse. My study mates seeing us go, went further away to enjoy their innocent games. He made me sit near him and took my hand, saying:

SAINT-ALMONT: Good Sainte-Alba, I owe you this testimony, and I think I've already rendered it to you in front of the whole seminary; you are the edification of the holy establishment whose superior I am. So why stubbornly refuse yourself the prize you have the right to win through your good conduct? Why not desire to enter holy orders? Good priests are becoming rare, and the Catholic Church needs good examples more than ever. Too much modesty might become a blameworthy fault.

AGATHA: Ah! My respected superior, my dear monsieur Saint-Almont, excuse this perhaps too-familiar expression in the mouth of the least worthy of your disciples...

SAINT-ALMONT: Far from offending me, my dear Sainte-Alba, it proves your trust in me; I have done nothing to lose it. Speak with all freedom.

AGATHA: All right! My dear superior, know that you judge me much too favorably.

SAINT-ALMONT: I don't think so. Nothing about you so far appears to belie the accuracy of the praise which I'm happy to give you on every occasion. You have gentleness of character, docility, the modesty of a well-born young girl: precious qualities that one looks for in vain in people of your age and who have lived in Paris.

AGATHA: All right! I must not deceive you further.

SAINT-ALMONT: What is this?

AGATHA: You don't know me.

SAINT-ALMONT: What?

AGATHA: I have imposed on you too long.

SAINT-ALMONT: Speak; we are alone.

AGATHA: I don't dare.

SAINT-ALMONT: Yes, dare. What do you fear from me?

AGATHA: I fear losing your respect completely. Alas! I need only pronounce one word for that to happen.

SAINT-ALMONT: Your timid young soul perhaps is making you see a monster where there is only a slight fault.

AGATHA: I wish.

SAINT-ALMONT: You alarm me. Speak.

AGATHA: First, I have a request to address to you.

SAINT-ALMONT: Go ahead.

AGATHA: Promise me that whatever the revelation that I am going to make, you will pardon me for it.

SAINT-ALMONT: You know, my child, that the confession of a grave fault considerably diminishes its weight.

AGATHA: What I have to confide in you is of a nature to obtain pardon from no one, not even from the most indulgent official of our religion.

SAINT-ALMONT: The God we serve has given us the example of the most exceeding indulgence.

AGATHA: Tell me once again that you will pardon your good young man. This is what you have called me for a long time, without suspecting your error.

SAINT-ALMONT: I promise.

AGATHA: All right, then know...

SAINT-ALMONT: Courage, good young man, my dear Sainte-Alba.

AGATHA: The word dies on my lips and I dare not raise my eyes to you.

SAINT-ALMONT: Confidence! Imagine that I am your father. Come, my child, give me your hand...How burning hot it is!

AGATHA: Know, then...Ah! I can't...

SAINT-ALMONT: Gather your scattered senses.

AGATHA: Very honored superior of an institution of learning, what would you think of a woman...

SAINT-ALMONT: You've apparently hidden from me an unfortunate passion, perhaps an ungrateful woman forced you into the seminary without a vocation.

AGATHA: It isn't that, my dear Saint-Almont, it's worse than that.

SAINT-ALMONT: You frighten me; but speak.

AGATHA: Chase me from your presence, from your holy house; I have brought scandal to it. And bad fortune, said our divine teacher, bad fortune to those through whom scandal comes. Woe, woe!

SAINT-ALMONT (aside): Delirium is carrying away this poor young man.

AGATHA: Oh, no, it is not delirium, it's remorse. What would you think of an audacious woman who, dressed as a man, introduced herself into your seminary?

SAINT-ALMONT: Unhappy boy, what have you said?

AGATHA: The truth! Punish me, chase me out, denounce this crime to God's justice and to men.

SAINT-ALMONT: Unhappy girl! And why this cross-dressing? What is the point of choosing a seminary, mine, as the theatre of this scandalous project?

AGATHA: Ah! Monsieur de Saint-Almont, you don't yet know the half of my crime.

SAINT-ALMONT: What am I hearing? And what am I going to learn?

AGATHA: Love...

SAINT-ALMONT: What! You came into a refuge of peace and innocence to bring the incendiary torch of the most ardent, the most imperious of the passions; you came to distract the young levites who are entrusted to me! What audacity! What sacrilege! Oh, God, pardon, if you can...

AGATHA: Ah, Saint-Almont, may your holy anger not make you commit an injustice toward me! By your grace, don't insult me, and do distinguish a weakness—criminal, no doubt—from a shameful abomination. No, I have never come into your establishment to corrupt your worthy students; know better the heart of a sensitive woman. Only one object drew me to your seminary, and this object, worthy in the virtues that seduced me with all the passion of a pure and burning heart, still does not know that I burn for him.

SAINT-ALMONT: Do not seek to palliate the enormity of your fault; don't belie the candor that I believed I had observed in you.

AGATHA: You weren't deceived, and what I'm saying is the proof of that. Yes, the one for whom I allowed myself the strangest of projects still doesn't know that he was loved by a woman, and would perhaps never have known if I had been able to restrain myself, if I had dared to go further and enter holy orders with a profane heart.

SAINT-ALMONT: You must not tell him; this secret can only be confided in me, who am charged with the moral guardianship of these ecclesiastics.

AGATHA: I can't any longer let suspicion fall on the young students of your establishment, for you could suppose me capable of making an incomplete or false revelation. So learn that none of them was the object of my fatal love.

SAINT-ALMONT: None of them!

AGATHA: None.

SAINT-ALMONT: Then who?

AGATHA: Do I still need to tell you that it is you, monsieur de Saint-Almont?

SAINT-ALMONT: Me!

AGATHA: Alas, yes, yourself. And how have you not guessed this sad confession, you who have loved so unhappily? It seems that heaven wanted to avenge your sex by punishing me for the faults of mine. Whatever my imprudence, my temerity, even my sacrilege, know, monsieur de Saint-Almont, that I believe myself far less guilty than the woman who, playing with your affection, forced you into the priesthood; you have no more vocation than I do.

SAINT-ALMONT: How do you know?

AGATHA: I knew about your misfortune; I came to know your virtues. Did I need more to attach myself to you, even without hope and without a goal? I never had any illusions. From the first instant that I loved you, I never pretended to myself that I could ever belong to you. But is anyone the ruler of love? Does anyone govern his destiny? Pity me, but don't degrade me.

SAINT-ALMONT: Why, unthinking woman, why come to my seminary?

AGATHA: I attended your first mass. From that time, more dangerous for me than for you, for you were entering the harbor while I was launching myself into a torrent; since that sad moment I vowed myself, so to speak, to you. I followed your every step. It's I whom you noticed so assiduous in the rituals where you officiated; it's I who went to request the presence of your holy ministry at the deathbed of my too indulgent grandmother; it's she who, far from foreseeing the consequences, allowed me to dress up in men's clothing; it's I...

SAINT-ALMONT: My daughter! I will do my duty; you will do yours.

AGATHA: I understand.

SAINT-ALMONT: You will feign a grave illness.

AGATHA: I won't have to feign.

SAINT-ALMONT: You will stay here; you will spend the night in the home of the caretaker of this establishment. Tomorrow, I will send back to you the deposit of the gold pieces you entrusted to me, and…

AGATHA: And…

SAINT-ALMONT: We will end every connection. My position, your sex…Unhappy woman! May Providence watch over you! Adieu; although it has to be me that brings you to the caretaker.

Here my existence ends, for I can only vegetate. Oh, my Zoé, what an ending! You tried to make me see it from the beginning. Let's finish the sacrifice. He left, leading his students; and I, I stayed in a room of the caretaker of the country house. Accept my last goodbye. A choking feeling takes away any ability to write you further. Tomorrow at dawn I leave this house to go I don't know where; but as I already indicated, neither you nor Saint-Almont will hear anything more of the unfortunate Agatha.

In a note I leave to be delivered to him, I ask him to collect this letter with a packet of others that he will find in an envelope in my seminary chamber, and to send everything to your address, at your former home, where those who write to your husband can leave their letters. Adieu, adieu, adieu, Zoé.

N.B. Saint-Almont returned the cash amount and the papers of the girl whom he had believed to be one of his neophytes, to the address she indicated. Two months later, Zoé returned and found all this at her former home. She wept for her friend, whom at first she thought she had lost forever.

✶ The publisher of this correspondence, just when he least expected it, received other information that will interest the reader curious to know what finally became of the unfortunate heroine of these Letters.

Agatha spent a terrible night in the caretaker's lodge at the seminary's country house. She left at dawn, before the time when Saint-Almont was to return the funds he had in trust; so that Agatha, who had on her only a few coins, found herself without the means to exchange her seminary clothes for those of her sex. So, still dressed as an ecclesiastic, she wandered in the neighboring fields with the intention of reaching the river. She revolved in her mind a sinister project, which she planned to act on.

Fortunately, in her delirium she lost her way and didn't dare ask directions. After two or three hours of rapid but aimless walking, she passed the entrance of an abandoned quarry located under the pleasant hill which separates the two beautiful villages of Ivri and Vitri-sur-Seine. Worn out by fatigue, exhausted by need, she turns her steps into the dark interior of this cavern hollowed out by men's hands, penetrates its depths, and lies down on a bed of stone. A deep sleep, or rather a trance, steals her senses and binds all her faculties.

This quarry, which the workers had mined out, was not deserted. It formed a network of chambers and went on a long way, lit now and then by openings or air holes connected to the surface of the neighboring countryside. One of these subterranean galleries ended at the cellars of a house in the next village, and this conduit served as the dwelling of an unusual character whom we will sketch for the eyes of our readers. We will call him Timon, or the modern misanthrope,[19] so as not to compromise anyone. This man, still young, had experienced a number of misfortunes and many more injustices. Gifted with a sensitive soul and a strong imagination, he was irresistibly attracted to philosophy, and to that of the Stoics above all. The world in which he lived had given him only too many opportunities to exercise his reflective spirit. His early youth had been studious. He had meditated on the most profoundly thoughtful books, and accordingly, he had constructed for himself a brilliant theory, but one above human power to implement, at least as long as the present social system remains in place. Our sage, at the passionate age, had the imprudence to wish to put into practice the exalted principles he had created for himself, and found nothing but resistance everywhere. His century was not sufficiently mature, and his country was too corrupt for the success of his bold and austere plans. Unworthily toyed with by women, outrageously pursued by the high clergy whose turpitude he did not fear to reveal in a book which made only too much of a sensation, our philosopher degenerated quickly into a misanthrope, withdrew from society, changed his name, and came to live under the thatched roof of a peasant in Vitri. The solitary life he led there did not cure him of his more or less well-founded antagonism toward the world. Investigating the area around his new home, he discovered one day an underground gallery abutting the parish where he lived. From then on, he broke all his connections and kept no other relations with his fellow humans than those required to not die of hunger. The good people with whom he lived and to whom he paid a good pension, armed with his power of attorney, took care of all his business and contradicted him in nothing. Rarely did he dine with them. He came himself to get his food, and went to eat it in the cavern connected to the cellar of his hosts. There he gave himself over to dark meditations, completely at leisure and without fearing busybodies. Sometimes he committed to paper his morose thoughts, or else inscribed on the smoothest walls of his quarry a few poems of the type of these stanzas:

MISANTHROPIC STANZAS.

Through your own fault, poor humans,
Oh, how many ills you endure on earth!
As for me, far from you, in a quarry pit,
I have found peace and rest.

Poor humans! You resemble the stones
That an architect, whether skilled or not,

With his fantastical or severe sketches
Places and displaces to please the reigning gods.

When I see you from the depth of my cavern,
Poor humans! you make me pity you.
Let someone else bow for a bit of gold!
I miss nothing here but friendship.

Yes, I prefer a cavern to the temples
Where the fakir gives a moral speech
Belied by his bad example.
Poor humans! you are captured by words.

With your kings, your republics,
Poor humans! are you happy? No.
Return instead to the peaceful laws
Of Nature; only she is right.

For ages it has been said that truth
Lives at the bottom of a well.
I have found it in the depths of my cave;
But I'd like to find love there, too.

    Timon thus busied himself with a reform of the human species, which he detested. The clergy was not spared in his virulent diatribes. And this is how he employed his days, wandering alone in the nooks and crannies of the quarry that had become a new world for him. Sometimes he spent entire nights writing his bitter observations in the light of a lamp. Too often his brain became inflamed and he would have been brought to violent excess if one of those he had only too much to complain about had been present. He had taken on an attitude of general defiance, not taking a step without having two pistols in his belt and a dagger.

With this formidable toolkit and in a moment of profound misanthropy, he spies, stretched out on the stone, an individual in ecclesiastical habit. Seeing this, he can't restrain himself! With one hand he raises his dagger; with the other he seizes the collar of the sleeping Agatha's robe. He grabs it with force, rips it, and bares part of the unfortunate woman's breast; she awakens with a sudden start, remaining immobile and mute at the surprising spectacle that strikes her eyes. Indeed, what must have been her terror seeing a man in a fur hat, a miner's lamp suspended from this hat, armed with pistols and a menacing knife, a savage eye, and his face in something like a convulsion!

But in recognizing a woman under the ecclesiastical costume, Timon himself doesn't know what to think; other sentiments mix with the indignation he felt at first. The dagger falls from his hand; the other releases Agatha's robe. He puts his two pistols on the ground, and is disconcerted in the presence of something so far from his thought.

Agatha, fallen back on the stone that served her as a couch, had fainted. Timon, meanwhile come back to himself, runs to the home of his hosts and brings back strong spirits, to administer some help to the girl he had so badly frightened. At last, when he was able to speak to her with poise, and she to hear him, he said:

> TIMON: Most imprudent girl! What are you looking for in these environs so little made for your age and your sex? Did you come to confront a man who has only too much to complain about from women and from those whose habit you wear? Tell me without any deceit, and be reassured; you have nothing to worry about from me. Have you merely escaped from some costume party? Up there, they dance, they amuse themselves, they play with their chains—those slaves of every prejudice! Did they chase you

from the party for having dared to wear the clergy's habit, jealous that it should only be the cleric who has the right to wear a mask? Answer.

AGATHA (scarcely brought back to herself): Alas! Monsieur…

TIMON: Don't call me "Monsieur!" I am not a polite Monsieur toward other people, and I'm tough because of misfortune; I have perhaps acquired a brusque character, but even if I no longer look like a man, I have maintained a soul sensitive to adversities. Might you have experienced some? Tell them to me.

AGATHA: I hope that I will soon arrive at their end. What's the use of discussing them with you?

TIMON: I want one more reason to hate humanity, even though I already have enough. But why this sinister disguise? I want to know. Ah! Apologies, unfortunate woman—probably more unfortunate than guilty. Right now I ought to be occupying myself only with your needs; first I will satisfy the most pressing of them. Promise me to wait; I am going to get some food necessary to your condition.

Agatha, weaker than Nature, which spoke more loudly than her unhappy passion, consented to accept nourishment. Quick as lightning, Timon left and returned, and both took a light meal served on a slab of stone.

TIMON: You stubbornly continue to be silent about your problems. Will you refuse to accept women's clothes in place of these? They are so unsuitable, even for men!

AGATHA: I will finish living and dying in this clothing; it is dear to me. Besides, I don't have long to wear it; a mortal blow has struck my heart.

Timon insisted so often that Agatha could not prevent herself from recounting the secret troubles that so strongly affected her.

Cursed social mores! (he exclaimed at this tale), false human respect! Oh, how men make themselves unhappy by their own deeds! Fooled by a flirt, Saint-Almont makes himself a priest, that is, he punishes himself for the faults of another. Then he reduces to despair the sensitive girl whom Nature brought him by the hand to make good the error he had committed with another so little worthy of him! How bizarre! What a reversal of every sane idea! Poor Agatha, I pity you. But stay here and don't die; remain in this quarry under the earth which is not worthy of having you on it. Forget Saint-Almont, in whom religious prejudice speaks louder than Nature. Stay here; you will be as secure as in your seminary and as free as you like; consent to live. Our reciprocal destiny is perhaps that we should live near one another, since we are both victims of those clever social conventions that enslave human beings.

AGATHA: I don't have your strength of spirit or physique to tolerate my adversity. I feel that the weight oppressing my heart can be relieved only by death; I'll languish for a few days more, happy to have found a compassionate hand to assist me in my last moments. Don't insist on calling me back to happiness. There are people apparently born to suffer; but at least I am not guilty, neither in men's eyes nor before my God. I have committed only imprudence.

TIMON: Don't speak to me of your God; he owes you a miracle.

AGATHA: He owes me nothing.

TIMON: Your God is unjust.

AGATHA: My God is just: in me he leaves an example from which young girls will be able to profit. They will be told

This is the only illustration in the only edition of Maréchal's novella, where it appears as the frontispiece. It portrays Timon's discovery of Agatha in his quarry. The engravers were Louis Binet and Edmé Bovinet.

(Courtesy Lilly Library, Indiana University.)

that I was punished for having neglected the wise counsel of a friend, and for having believed nothing but my inexperienced heart.

TIMON: You have followed the voice of Nature, who never deceives, but your religions and your laws contradict her. It's they that do all the evil. Ah! When will people retrace their steps, return to their primitive social organization, and learn how to live without the ridiculous and sinister scaffolding of either political or sacred legislation? How I despise, how I hate all these ancient and modern legislators who, substituting their false reasonings for reason, invent the snares in which the rest of mankind, like lowly sheep, come to be caught! It is no longer permitted for the young, innocent virgin to be united with the young man into whose arms Nature impels her, but absurd codes, imagined by ambitious people, forbid her by all kinds of miserable rules.

These declamations relieved Timon and reassured Agatha. He limited himself to apostrophes of highborn men, without neglecting the respect due to the passion and the sex of the unfortunate girl. She, languishing and gradually growing weaker, had given up any attempt on her own life; resigned, she saw approaching the last day of a life short but full of bitterness.

Timon, busy nearby, hoped and expected everything from the passage of time; already his imagination let him glimpse a happy future according to his principles. One day, he approaches Agatha with an urgency more marked than usual, in order to say:

Unhappy woman! Without doubt you do me justice; I have fulfilled the duties of hospitality toward you, without attaching a price as they do up there. Have I earned some rights to your trust?

AGATHA: Generous man, can you doubt it?

TIMON: All right, then give me proof.

AGATHA: You worry me. Are you getting tired of being virtuous?

TIMON: You don't understand. Listen to me until I'm done. The interior of a quarry is unhealthy, especially for people already weakened by a violent attack of passion. Why should you stay here any longer?

AGATHA: To die more quickly.

TIMON: Still this sinister image in view! I have something better to propose. Perhaps I express myself in terms that echo of this cavern I inhabit rather than of the surface of the earth that is soiled by so many crimes; but do me the favor of courtesy and judge only my intentions, which are as pure as the love you bore Saint-Almont.

AGATHA: And which I will maintain until my last breath.

TIMON: All these considerations can very well be reconciled. Lend me all your attention; what I have to say deserves it. You will agree, I think, that whatever happens above our heads is marked somewhere with folly or perversity. Women are either deceived or deceivers; men oppressed or oppressors. The finest cities offer only traps for honest people and are evil places for others. The more populous they are, the more crimes and misfortunes are in them. Retreat to the countryside is hardly more secure or more innocent—people there are a little less wicked because a little more ignorant.

Every day I bless the happy moment when I was inspired to break with the whole human species and bury myself in the bowels of the earth. Agatha, you also should bless that unhappy passion that brought you here. You needed a world more capable of appreciating your innocence and your loving soul. You need a still-virgin corner of earth where vice and prejudice have not penetrated, such as exists, we are assured, beyond the sea, in the forests of North America. I still have enough property for the expenses of this voyage and for the advance costs of the little colony I have in mind, in the vicinity of the good Quakers, of all people the ones who have degenerated least. Come, your health and your peace depend on this decision. The dangerous animals of those countries are less dangerous than our European compatriots. We both have plenty of reasons to flee a society that only claims to be civil, and to make a separate one on earth. Come with me, unfortunate Agatha; come found a colony as virtuous as yourself but happier.

AGATHA: A longer voyage is prescribed for me; I feel its approach in the weakness I experience; I will precede in a better world the man who is dear to me and with whom I wasn't able to spend my life in this lower world. Accept the testimony of all my gratitude for the benevolent opinion you have of me but which I can't profit from.

TIMON: Well, what is preventing you, obstinate girl?

AGATHA: A doe who bears in her flank the spear with which she has been wounded can't go any further.

TIMON: So you don't want to reconcile me with the human species?

AGATHE: I can't.

TIMON: Was I wrong to be a misanthrope and to curse this globe where I have lived too long? Prejudices of every kind! you have flooded the earth with all the evils that overwhelm it, and it's still you that prevent its return to the good. Stubborn Agatha! Think about the happy consequences of the proposition I've risked making to you. Transport yourself mentally to a climate no less mild than that of France, and on a soil still intact, and perfectly alien to everything that wounds our hearts and our eyes amidst this complicated civilization of which you still know only the most minor troubles. Imagine strolling with me amid beautiful forests, where noble savages will build us a dwelling without luxury but healthy and tranquil. We will establish ourselves there without difficulty; we will turn without anxiety to the sweet inclinations of nature, and we will forget the old world so as not to curse it. Soon a posterity offers a support in our old age. Our little family becomes for us a whole universe. We live satisfied, without feeling any need for a code and a religion. Maternal tenderness and filial piety are our only divinities. What a picture! And is so much needed to make it real? Agatha, you still have enough health for this voyage; consent to breathe a purer air and place your trust in a man who deserves it.

AGATHA: Yes, no doubt you deserve it, but these too-sweet illusions can find no place in a soul bowed down by sorrow. Spare me more refusals; leave me to the painful situation you found me in; no one can pull me out of it. Only death or God is capable of breaking the bonds I've undertaken.

TIMON: So wrong. Stubborn woman! Why did you come to trouble the peace I enjoyed here, and that I had bought with so many sacrifices? Why did your sudden appearance rekindle in my heart the flame of desire?

AGATHA: Ah! Don't reproach me with another fault, just as involuntary as the others.

TIMON: Excuse that unjust impulse, which I couldn't control.

AGATHA: So was I born under a fatal star?

TIMON: Not more fatal than mine.

AGATHA: But Providence is even stronger, and has applied balm to the deep wound I caused myself. Otherwise I could die even more guilty and more unhappy.

TIMON: These feeble and timorous souls think they've said everything when they've spoken the word "Providence." Providence! What does it do? Where is it? Why doesn't it foresee crime, or punish it? Why is it so rigorous toward Agatha and the few like her, yet so flexible for the women like those who have deceived me or the one who toyed with the tenderness of Saint-Almont? Providence! It's only a word.

AGATHA: Don't blaspheme.

TIMON: Let Providence justify itself!

AGATHA: Doubtless it will in a better world.

TIMON: All right! I will bless it at the right time; I will bless it from now on if it opens your heart to the propositions I've made you. Providence! There isn't any, or there is only for the wicked; only they prosper. The good languish like you, or are obliged, in order to exist in peace, to live like a bear like me. Providence! What wrong this word has done to honest people! It has counseled them resignation; it is the reason they don't form a powerful organization to oppose the scoundrels. The scoundrels profit from piety about Providence, and enjoy with impunity the advantages which ought to be the reward of virtue.

Despairing his unsuccessful attempt, Timon withdrew with somber sadness, and in the following days he spoke no more of his project, but redoubled his caring attention to Agatha. In order to be sure that no haphazard nuisance could visit, he blocked with stones the quarry entrance through which the unfortunate girl had penetrated the interior. He got wood to combat the humidity of the gallery where Agatha had established herself; already he had brought weavings and rugs.

But alas! all these efforts could scarcely lengthen the fabric of Agatha's days. Timon saw her weaken slowly, but without sharp pain, like a torch that dies down little by little. The profound sorrow she felt was enough, and at each perceptible step of this deterioration, Timon renewed his imprecations against Providence. Only the gentleness of the sick girl could temper them; he himself was astonished at the authority he allowed her over his spirit; but he didn't complain about it.

One evening, poor Agatha held out her hand to him, saying: "My generous host, since you no longer wish to recognize a God, I beg your own heart to bear witness to all the gratitude I owe you. Add to it the last service I will ask of you. Procure what I need to write a letter, and grant me the grace of making sure it gets to its address, without bothering about the choice of the person whose good offices I claim along with yours."

TIMON: I foresee what you are thinking of, but I can't refuse you anything. Write.

THE LETTER: "Monsieur de Saint-Almont is begged to accompany the officer who presents this letter. He cannot refuse this last grace to the unfortunate Agatha de Sainte-Alba who is dying."

TIMON: You forget the address.

AGATHE: I don't have enough strength to write it. Lend me the help of your hand; mine trembles too much. "To Monsieur the abbé de Saint-Almont, superior of the seminary."

TIMON: But, always careless Agatha! You aren't thinking that you put me at the mercy of a priest.

AGATHA: This one has only the virtues of a priest. We will make him promise not to divulge the secret of your refuge, and he won't violate his word.

TIMON: Who can assure me of that? For after all, he is a priest.

AGATHA: Up to now you've seemed to respect me a bit. Sacrifice your premonitions, and deign to judge me worthy of some trust.

Timon insisted no further. The next day, he reappeared with this response to the letter of the previous night.

Zoé to her dear Agatha.

"My completely good and unfortunate friend! I looked for you everywhere, with the solicitude of a mother who has lost her cherished child. Finally, I find you, and doubtless soon you will allow me to enclose you in my arms. Monsieur de Saint-Almont is no longer superior at the seminary, nor even in Paris. He asked to be part of a mission to the savages of northern America. Our ships crossed paths. As he was going to the new world, I was coming back from it with my husband, who was as worried as myself about our dear Agatha. Your letter has been brought to your old friends, who already possessed your journal and the rest of what belonged to you. We await with impatience the moment when we will embrace you."

This letter, received suddenly and with no preparation, caused a revolution in what doctors call "the nervous system" and would have hastened Agatha's last moment without the redoubled care of Timon. When this crisis had passed, Agatha, who could no longer write by herself, had Zoé sent for, whom she awaited with an impatience equal to her friend's. Zoé hurried to her the next day, accompanied by her husband. The two good friends held one another tightly, without being able to express in words what they felt; but this sweet embrace of friendship said more.

Warned of Agatha's exhausted condition, Zoé had come prepared with a medication composed by the savages of Canada and famous in that country for its marvelous cures; but this prescription came too late. Administered a little sooner, it might have called her back to life. The unfortunate girl was unable to resist the stress of meeting her old friend; she expired in her arms, the second day of their reunion in the quarry.

Timon became only more misanthropic; he crossed the ocean with Zoé and her husband when they returned to northern America. There, Timon obtained from the savage forest dwellers permission to spend the rest of his days with them. He embraced their way of life with such success that they regarded him as a brother, and had limitless trust in him. This circumstance saved Saint-Almont's life. Some Iroquois whose conversion he had undertaken turned against him and were going to hack him to pieces, believing him a spy sent by the English. As chance would have it, Timon, hunting at the head of his adopted tribe, recognized the superior of poor Agatha's seminary. He obtained his ransom and led him to Zoé's household, where Saint-Almont lived henceforth, renouncing the priesthood and devoting himself to the education of the only son of the household.

Every year, Timon came to spend a week with them, to commemorate the unhappy love and the death of Agatha. Returning to his kindly savages, he repeated this verse from the misanthropic ballad cited above:

With your kings and republics,
Poor humans! are you happy? No.
Instead, return to the peaceful laws
Of Nature: only she is right.

THE END.

Notes

Introduction

1. For French medieval tales, see, among others, "Le roman de Silence" and "Le roi Flore et la belle Jehane," both thirteenth century, both treated (along with two others) by Dietzman; also Delany, "Flore et Jehane"; edition in Jacob. For berdache or two-spirit people, see Lang as well as Roscoe; for Oman, see Wikan; for Europe, see Friedli as well as Dekker and van de Pol.
2. See Cordingly, especially Chapters 4 and 5; Stark; and Wheelwright on women (mostly British, some American) at sea. For a mid-nineteenth-century American instance, see the "Narrative" of Lucy Ann Lobdell. For current instances, see Attenberg; and Nordberg on girls raised as boys in Afghanistan.
3. On August 24, 1572, feast day of St. Bartholomew, Protestants in Paris were massacred by Catholics. Only in 1598 with the Edict of Nantes was freedom of worship allowed; this was revoked in 1685 until civil rights were restored over a century later during the French Revolution. Carmelites were an order of nuns and mendicant friars, taking their name from Mt. Carmel in Palestine. Maréchal's all-female legendary is in alphabetical order by saint's name.
4. See Molinier, *Catalogue des manuscrits de la Bibliothèque Mazarine*. Despite the title, most items are not in manuscript form; many are nearly contemporary.

The Woman Priest

1. Éloi-Nicholas-Marie Miroir was organist at several Parisian churches between 1780 and 1815. He was sufficiently well thought of by the revolutionary government to serve on a 1795 commission with two other organists to examine the great organ at Saint-Germain-l'Auxerrois, which had been transferred from Sainte-Chapelle du Palais in 1791. In the next century, F.-J. Fétis wrote, concerning organ music, of the "special effects, tonal contrasts...and ways to

arouse and gratify sensual instincts....When I was young, a certain M. Miroir enjoyed a great reputation for that kind of wizardry."

2. levite: In the Hebrew bible, the assistant priests were the levites. Maréchal published his study of the Hebrew and Christian bibles, *Pour et contre la bible*, in the same year as *La femme abbé*.

3. *Dominus vobiscum*: The lord [be] with you.

4. The French has "état," which, at the pre-revolutionary time in which the story is set, would refer to one of the three main divisions of French society: clergy, aristocracy, and middle class (the first, second, and third estates, respectively). The young man's name indicates that he is of the second estate, but he has now chosen to enter the first.

5. "Paris vaut bien une messe." Henry IV, king of France (1589–1610), twice abjured the Protestantism he was raised with in order to take the French throne, which was limited to Catholics. On one of these occasions, he is alleged to have made the remark quoted by Agatha.

6. meat-eating days: The Catholic Church designates fasting days and days on which it is permitted to eat meat. The three days before Ash Wednesday (the start of Lent, a period of deprivation leading up to Easter) are meat-eating, or "fat" (*gras*) days; hence *Mardi gras* or, literally, fat Tuesday.

7. penitentiary: an experienced priest designated by the bishop to deal with special cases requiring absolution. In an extremely serious case, this might be a cardinal appointed by the pope.

8. *lavabo*: Latin, I will wash. From Psalm 26,6: I wash my hands in innocence. Spoken by the priest as he dips his fingers in water at the start of the service.

9. enjoyment: the French has "jouissance," which can (but need not) mean pleasure of a sexual nature.

10. Sacchini: Antonio Sacchini (1730–1786), Italian opera composer; he died in Paris. A number of his many operas were on classical themes, and the classics-loving Maréchal would likely have been a fan.

11. *oremus*: Latin, Let us pray.

12. aspersion: sprinkling with holy water, a ritual performed by the priest.

13. carnival: The period of merry-making just preceding the privations of Lent, the forty days preceding Easter. During Lent, Catholics are supposed to give up something, perhaps fast during the days or eat no meat.

14. Mentor-Zoé: in the *Odyssey*, an old man who gives the hero good advice, as Zoé does for Agatha.

15. director: that is, spiritual director, a role which for Catholics can only be filled by a priest.

16. louis: a gold coin named after a king of France, Louis XIII (d. 1643), whose image adorned it.
17. paten: small dish on which the host, or consecrated wafer, is laid during communion.
18. priestly: because it commemorates the establishment of the Eucharist, which has to be administered by a priest.
19. misanthrope: Timon of Athens, eponymous character of Shakespeare's play, was famously misanthropic.

Bibliography

Andrès, Bernard. "De Montréal aux échelles du Levant." *Cahiers de la Méditeranée* 75 (2007): 133-43.

Arden, Heather, ed. *Medievalism in France, 1500-1750*. Special issue of *Studies in Medievalism* 3 (1987).

Attenberg, Jami. "Track Changes." *New York Times Sunday Magazine*, January 25, 2015, 54.

Aubert, Françoise. *Sylvain Maréchal. Passion et faillite d'un égalitaire*. Pisa: Goliardica; Paris: Nizet, 1975.

Bastien, J.-F., trans. *Lettres d'Abailard et d'Héloïse*. 2 vol. Paris: Chez l'Editeur, 1782.

Boucher, Philip P. *Les Nouvelles-Frances. La France en Amérique, 1500-1815*. Sillery, QC: Septentrion, 2004.

Bouvier, Jeanne. *Les femmes pendant la Révolution*. Paris: Figuère, 1931.

Champlain, Samuel de. *Des sauvages*. Edited by Alain Beaulieu and Réal Ouellet. Montreal: Typo, 1993.

Charlevoix, F.-X. de. *Textes choisis et présentés par Léon Pouliot*. Montreal and Paris: Fides, 1959.

Cizewski, Wanda. "From Historia Calamitatum to Amours et infortunes." In Arden, 71-76.

Cordingly, David. *Women Sailors & Sailors' Women: An Untold Maritime History*. New York and Toronto: Random House, 2001.

Dale, Ronald J. *The Fall of New France: How the French Lost a North American Empire, 1754-1763*. Toronto: Lorimer, 2004.

Dekker, Rudolf M., and Lotte C. van de Pol. *The Tradition of Female Transvestism in Early Modern Europe*. New York: Palgrave Macmillan, 1989.

Delany, Sheila. "Afterlife of a Medieval Genre: The *Nouvelle légende dorée* (1790) of Sylvain Maréchal," *Exemplaria* 22, no. 1 (2010): 28-43.

———. "Flore et Jehane: A Case Study of the Bourgeois Woman in Medieval Life and Letters." *Science and Society* 45, no. 3 (1981): 274–87.

———. "St. Genevieve in the Revolution: Sylvain Maréchal's Counter-History." In *Les saints et la sainteté*, ed. Jean-Phillipe Plez and Jean-Baptiste Decherf, special issue of *Conserveries mémorielles* 14 (2013). www.cm.revues.org/1645.

Dietzman, Sara Jane. "En guize d'omme: Female Cross-Dressing and Gender Reversal in Four Medieval French Texts." PHD diss., University of Virginia, 2005.

Dommanget, Maurice. *Sur Babeuf et la conjuration des égaux*. Paris: Maspero, 1970.

———. *Sylvain Maréchal l'égalitaire*. Paris: Spartacus, 1950.

Douthwaite, Julia. *The Frankenstein of 1790 and Other Lost Chapters from Revolutionary France*. Chicago: University of Chicago Press, 2012.

Dubois, Laurent. *Avengers of the New World: The Story of the Haitian Revolution*. Cambridge, MA: Harvard University Press, 2004.

Eccles, W.J. *Canadian Society during the French Regime*. Montreal: Harvest House, 1968.

———. *Essays on New France*. Toronto: Oxford University Press, 1987.

———. *The French in North America, 1500-1783*. Rev. ed. Markham, ON: Fitzhenry and Whiteside, 1998.

———. *The Government of New France*. Ottawa: Canadian Historical Society, 1965.

Edelman, Nathan. *Attitudes of Seventeenth-Century France toward the Middle Ages*. New York: King's Crown Press, 1946.

Farge, Arlette. *Vivre dans la rue à Paris au XVIIIe siècle*. 1979. Paris: Gallimard, 1992.

Fétis, F.-J. "L'orgue mondaine et la musique érotique à l'église." *Revue et gazette musicale*, April 6, 1856.

Friedli, Lynne. "'Passing Women': A Study of Gender Boundaries in the Eighteenth Century." In *Sexual Underworlds of the Enlightenment*, ed. G.S. Rousseau and Roy Porter, 234–60. Manchester: Manchester University Press, 1987.

Fusil, Charles. *Sylvain Maréchal, ou l'homme sans dieu, H.S.D., 1750-1803*. Paris: Librairie Plon, 1936.

Gelbart, Nina Rattner. *Feminine and Opposition Journalism in Old Regime France: "Le journal des dames."* Berkeley: University of California Press, 1987.

Heldris of Cornwall. *Silence: A Thirteenth-Century French Romance*. Translated and edited by Sarah Roche-Mahdi. East Lansing, MI: Colleagues Press, 1992.

Jacob, Eliane. "'Le conte du roi Flore et la belle Jehane.' Roman d'aventure de prose." PHD diss., University of Strasbourg, 1972.

Jameson, Fredric. *The Political Unconscious : Narrative as a Socially Symbolic Act.* Ithaca, NY: Cornell University Press, 1981.

Lang, Sabine. *Men as Women, Women as Men: Changing Gender in Native American Cultures.* Austin: University of Texas, 1998.

Leclerq, Chrestien. *Nouvelle relation de la Gaspésie.* Edited by Réal Ouellet. Montreal: Presses de l'université de Montréal, 1999.

Lescarbot, Marc. *Spectacle of Empire: Marc Lescarbot's Theatre of Neptune in New France.* Edited by Jerry Wasserman. Vancouver: Talonbooks, 2006.

———. *Voyages en Acadie, suivis de la description des mœurs souriquoises comparées à celles d'autres peuples.* Edited by Marie-Chrisine Pioffet. Quebec: Presses de l'Université Laval, 2007.

Lévi-Strauss, Claude. *Tristes tropiques: An Anthropological Study of Primitive Societies in Brazil.* 1955. Translated by John Russell. New York: Atheneum, 1967.

Lobdell, Bambi. *A Strange Sort of Being: The Transgender Life of Lucy Ann/Joseph Israel Lobdell.* Jefferson, NC: McFarland, 2012.

Mannucci, Erica Joy. *Finalmente il popolo pensa. Sylvain Maréchal nell'immagine della Rivoluzione francese.* Napoli: Guida, 2012.

Maréchal, Sylvain. *Almanach des honnêtes gens. L'an du premier regne de la raison.* [Paris, 1789].

———. *Calendrier des républicains.* Paris: Gueffier, 1793.

———. *Costumes civils actuels de tous les peuples connus, dessinés d'après nature, gravés et coloriés, Accompagnés d'une Notice Historique sur leurs Coutumes, Moeurs, Religions, &c. &c.* Paris: Pavard, 1788.

———. *Nouvelle légende dorée, ou Dictionnaire des saintes.* 2 vol. Rome [Paris], 1790. Translated with an Introduction by Sheila Delany as *Anti-Saints: The New Golden Legend* of Sylvain Maréchal. Edmonton: University of Alberta Press, 2012.

———. *Pour et contre la Bible.* Jerusalem [Paris], 1801.

McMullen, Lorraine. *An Odd Attempt in a Woman: The Literary Life of Frances Brooke.* Vancouver: University of British Columbia Press, 1983.

Molinier, Auguste, ed. *Catalogue des manuscrits de la Bibliothèque Mazarine.* 4 vol. Paris: Plon, 1885–98.

Montoya, Alicia C. *Medievalist Enlightenment from Charles Perrault to Jean-Jacques Rousseau.* Cambridge: D.S. Brewer, 2013.

Nordberg, Jenny. *The Underground Girls of Kabul: In Search of a Hidden Resistance in Afghanistan.* New York: Crown Publishers, 2014.

Perovic, Sanja. *The Calendar in Revolutionary France: Perceptions of Time in Literature, Culture, Politics*. Cambridge: Cambridge University Press, 2012.

Plank, Geoffrey. *An Unsettled Conquest: The British Campaign against the People of Acadia*. Philadelphia: University of Pennsylvania, 2001.

Roscoe, Will. *Changing Ones: Third and Fourth Genders in Native North America*. New York: St. Martin's Press, 1998.

Roy, Pierre-Georges. "La demoiselle Esther Brandeau à Québec." In *La ville de Québec sous le régime français*. 2 vol. Quebec: Service des Archives du Gouvernement de la province de Québec, 1930.

Rutebeuf. "Le dit de Frère Denise le Cordelier." In *Oeuvres complètes*, vol. 1, ed. M. Zink. Paris: Classiques Garnier, 1989.

Stark, Suzanne J. *Female Tars: Women Aboard Ship in the Age of Sail*. Annapolis, MD: Naval Institute Press, 1996.

Streeter, Harold Wade. *The Eighteenth Century English Novel in French Translation: A Bibliographical Study*. New York: Benjamin Blom, 1970.

Varin de la Marre. "Report to the Authorities in France, September 15, 1738." In *The Tale-Teller*, by Susan Glickman. Markham, ON: Cormorant Books, 2012.

Wheelwright, Julie. *Amazons and Military Maids: Women Who Dressed as Men in Pursuit of Life, Liberty and Happiness*. London: Pandora, 1989.

Wikan, Unni. *Behind the Veil in Arabia: Women in Oman*. Baltimore and London: Johns Hopkins University Press, 1982.

Yalom, Marilyn. *Blood Sisters: The French Revolution in Women's Memory*. New York: Basic Books, 1993.

Zezula, Jindrich. "Scholarly Medievalism in Renaissance France." In Arden, 11–20.

Other Titles from The University of Alberta Press

Anti-Saints
The *New Golden Legend* of Sylvain Maréchal
SHEILA DELANY
184 pages | Scholarly introduction, notes, bibliography
978-0-88864-604-0 | $34.95 paper
978-0-88864-791-7 | $27.99 PDF
Hagiography | French Revolution | Feminism

Locating the Past/Discovering the Present
Perspectives on Religion, Culture, and Marginality
DAVID GAY & STEPHEN R. REIMER, Editors
224 pages | B&W photographs, bibliography, index
978-0-88864-499-2 | $39.95 paper
978-0-88864-685-9 | $31.99 PDF
Religious Studies | Cultural Studies

The Measure of Paris
STEPHEN SCOBIE
356 pages | B&W photographs, index
Wayfarer series
978-0-88864-533-3 | $29.95 paper
978-0-88864-588-3 | $23.99 EPUB
978-0-88864-651-4 | $23.99 Amazon Kindle
978-0-88864-783-2 | $23.99 PDF
Literary Nonfiction | Cultural Studies | Memoir